CW01208755

THE
Magical Life
OF THE
Lotus-Born

Sherab Chödzin Kohn

AFTERWORD BY
Dzongsar Khyentse

ILLUSTRATED BY
Thinley Dorji

bala kids

CONTENTS

1. A Very Special Child   5

2. The Wish-Fulfilling Gem   9

3. Lotus-Born   15

4. The Prince's Mishap   19

5. The Charnel Ground   23

6. A Dakini Visits   29

7. Back in the World of the Living   35

8. The Lake of Fire   41

9. The Great Debate   47

10. The Land of Snows   53

11. The King's Plan   59

12. Master Bodhisattva   65

13. An Invitation   71

14. Lotus-Born Arrives   77

15. Samye Is Built   83

16. The Ministers' Deceit   87

17. Lotus-Born's Legacy   93

Afterword by Dzongsar Khyentse Rinpoche   99

Phonetic Guide   103

Publisher's Note   106

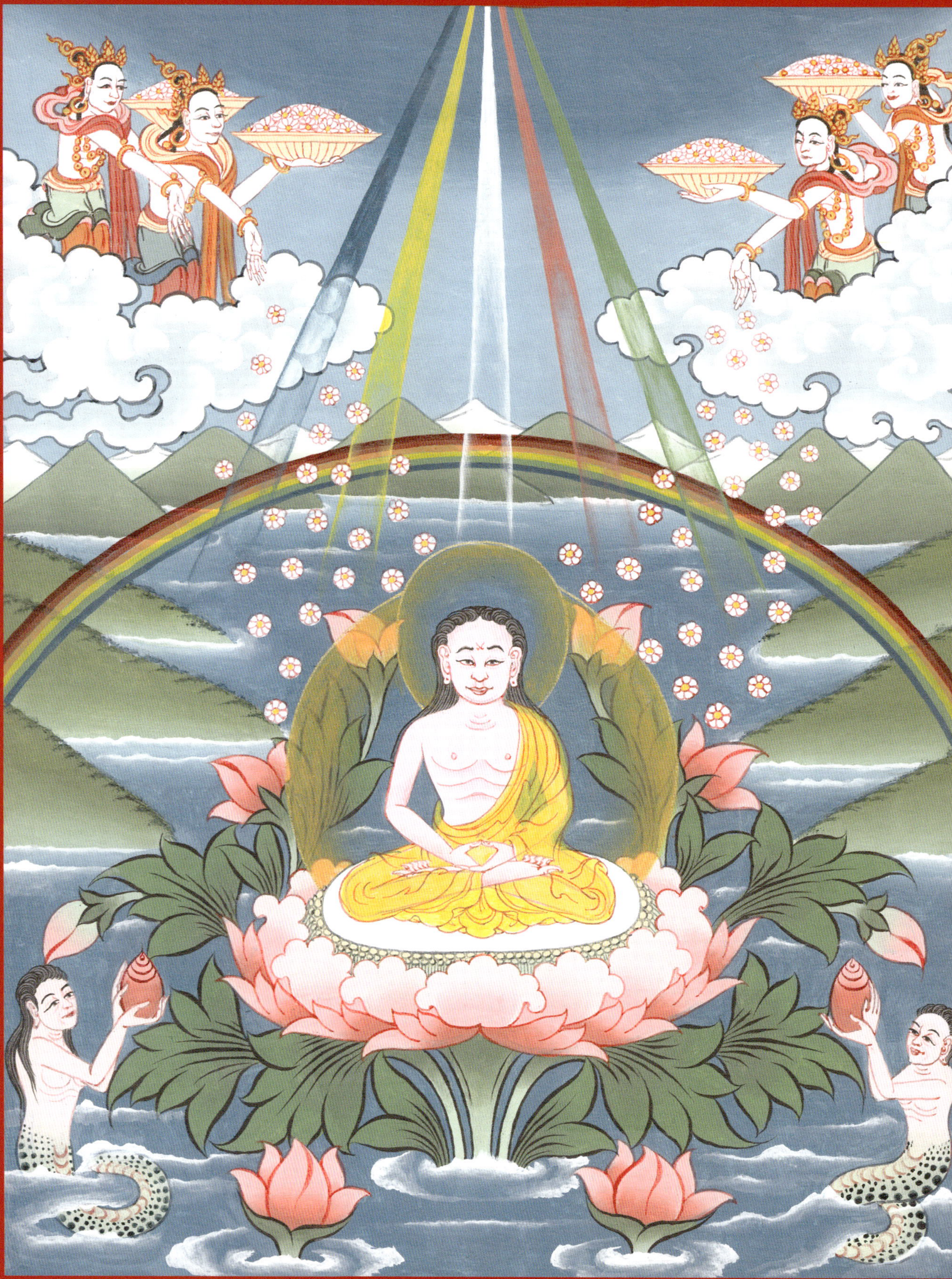

1

A VERY SPECIAL CHILD

Once upon a time, all the buddhas in the heavenly realm, in an effort to heal the troubles and suffering of the world, decided to form all their blessings and good wishes into one great sphere of rainbow light. That great sphere, like a shining egg, glowed and throbbed, extended outward, and turned into a brilliant ray of five colors that shone down through all the heavens until it reached the earth. There it fell upon a very big, pure white lotus flower growing in a lake on an island. When the ray touched the lotus, it changed again and turned into a radiantly beautiful child. The child sat quietly, smiling slightly, among the pure white petals of the huge flower.

Far, far away from the island where the lotus grew, in the kingdom of Odiyana, was a king named Indrabhuti who had fallen into great misfortune. He was a kind and generous king who had always given away his gold and treasure to feed the poor and hungry people of his kingdom. But now two things were making him very sad. First of all, he did not have any children—there was no one to inherit his kingdom. And second, his treasury was empty. He had given away all his riches and no longer had anything to give to the poor people who gathered daily at his palace gate. The king felt sorry for his poor subjects, because he loved them as though they were his own children. And he was also upset because they were angry at him for not taking care of them the way he always had.

The unhappy king decided to talk over the situation with his wife, the queen. He often talked to her when he needed advice, because she was a wise woman, and indeed she had a solution. She explained her idea to the king, who then called his ministers and courtiers together. He told them: "As you know, the treasury is empty. I have nothing to give to the poor, and also we have no money to pay for the other needs of the kingdom. We can't go on like this. But the queen has told me of a wondrous jewel that makes all wishes come true. If we had that, we could fill our treasury again with all the gold, silver, and jewels we will ever need. The Wish-Fulfilling Gem exists far away on an island in the great ocean. It is kept by the princess of the *nagas*, the gods of the sea and of all waters. The nagas possess tremendous wealth. The Wish-Fulfilling Gem is only one of their treasures, and I'm sure the princess will give it to us if Her Majesty and I speak to her humbly and truthfully and explain to her that we need it to help the poor. There is a ship in our harbor with a captain who has sailed the ocean many times and is wise in its ways. He will take us to the island of the princess of the nagas."

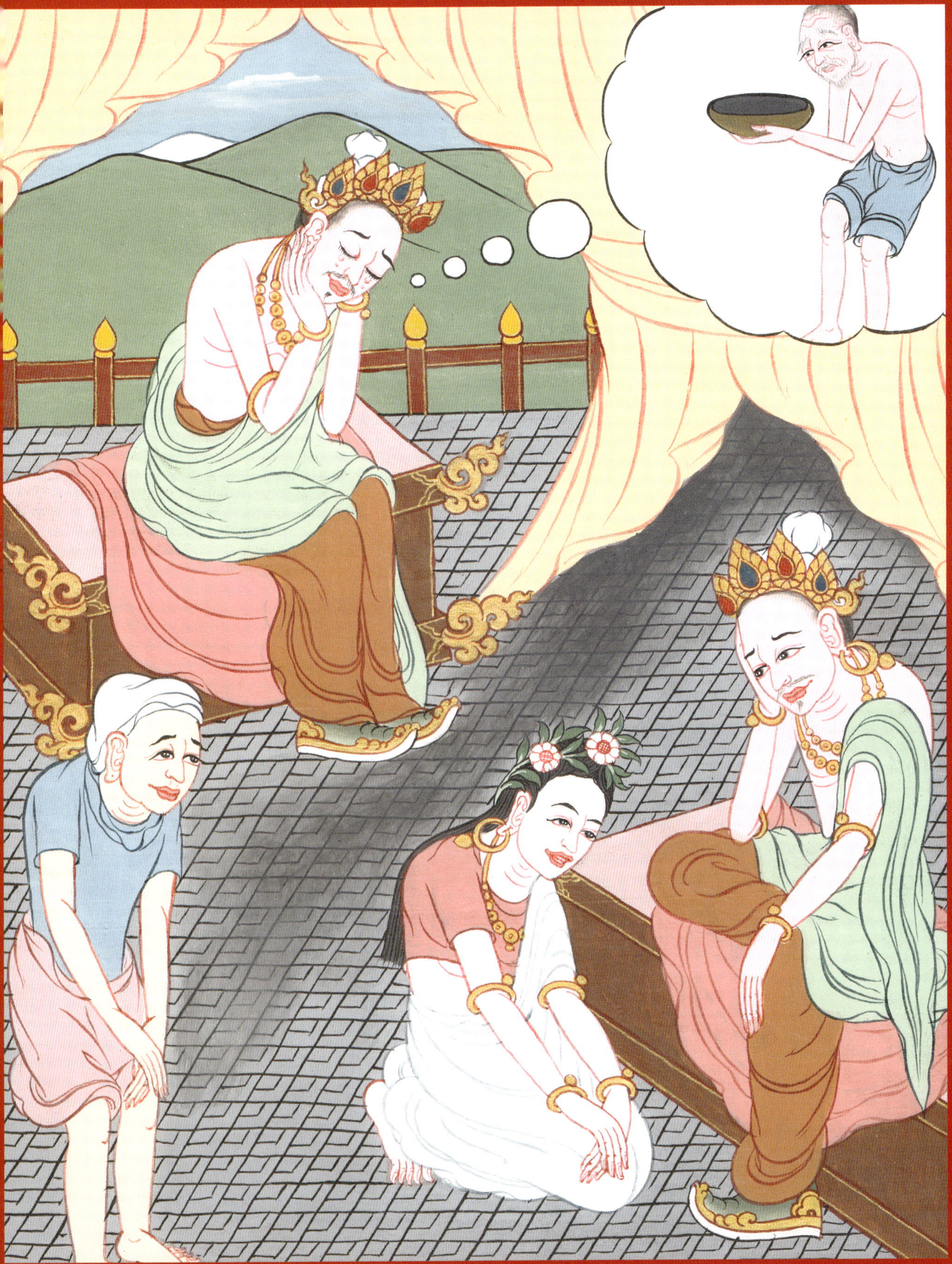

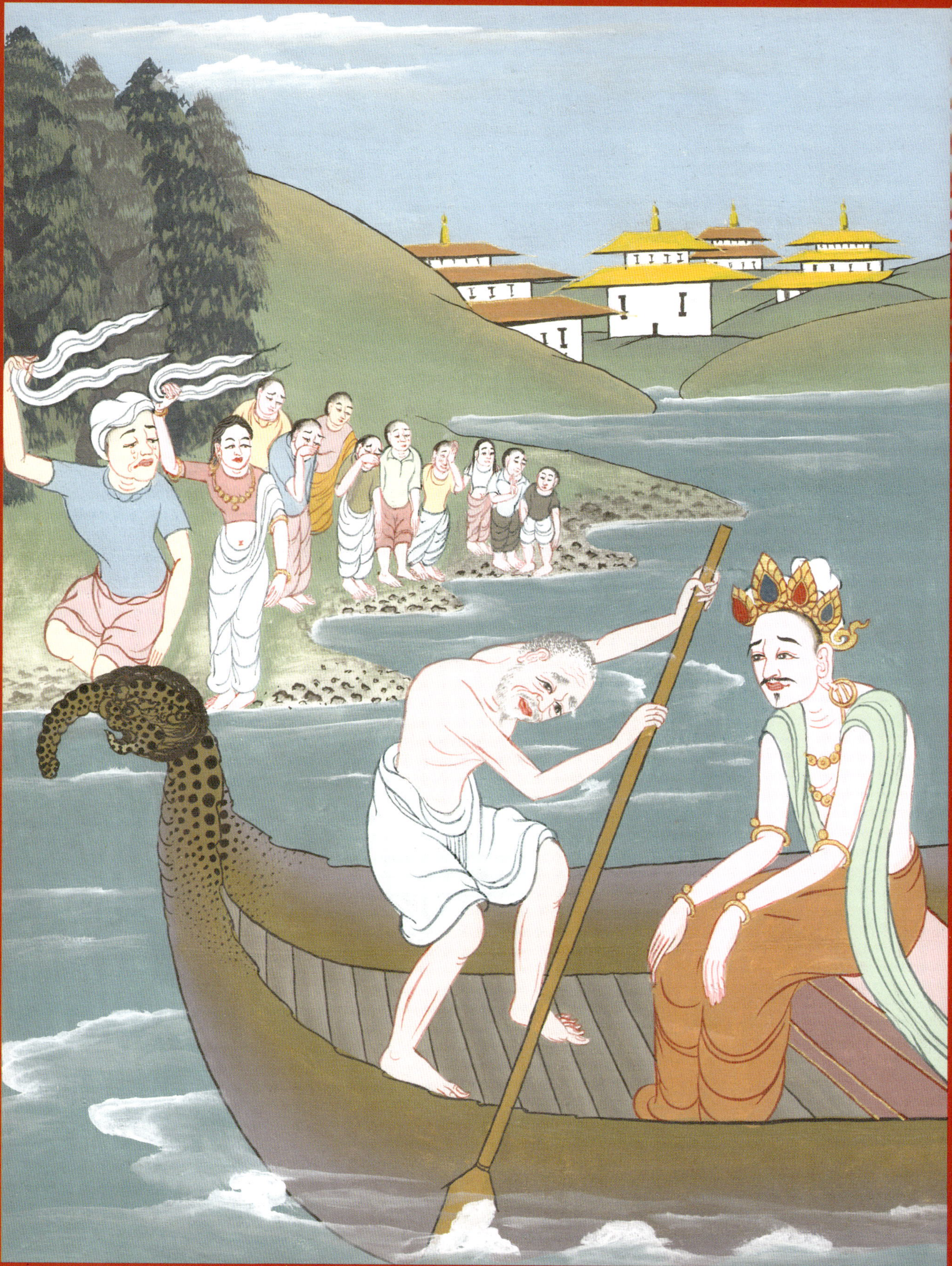

2

THE WISH-FULFILLING GEM

The next morning, the king and queen went down to the harbor and boarded the ship. All the people of Odiyana came to see them off and wish them well. A wind came up and filled their sails, and the people cheered as the ship sped away over the waves as fast as a speeding arrow. It wasn't long before it was pitching and rolling on the waves in the middle of the great ocean. When the wind blew in the right direction, the captain let the ship sail. When the wind blew in any other direction, he dropped his sails and lowered his anchors to keep the ship from moving. In this way, the ship sailed toward the island of the princess of the nagas, who possessed the Wish-Fulfilling Gem.

After many days on the sea they approached the island. The first thing the king and queen saw was a big white mountain.

"What is that big white mountain that is glowing so brightly?" asked the king.

"That is a mountain of silver," said the captain.

Next, they saw a mountain of pure blue that held the sunlight deep within it.

"What is that?" the king asked.

"Why, that is a mountain of sapphire," the captain said.

Next, a mountain of softly glowing yellow came into sight.

"What is that beautiful mountain?" asked the queen.

"That, Your Majesty, is a mountain of pure gold," the captain told her. "It is very close to the palace of the naga princess. We are almost there."

They anchored near the mountain of gold, where the sand of the beach itself was made of grains of gold. On a hill not far away from the shore was a castle made of precious stones.

"That is the castle of the princess of the nagas," the captain told the royal couple. "You must go on alone from here."

"The castle is surrounded by seven moats," the captain continued. "First you must get across those. Then you will reach an area full of poisonous snakes. If you get beyond that, you will come to the door of the castle. On the door is a knocker in the form of a golden thunderbolt. Knock on the door with that, and the naga princess herself will come and open the door."

"Good luck!" said the captain. "I'm sure you will succeed."

In a day and a night of fearsome struggles, the king and queen crossed the seven moats, and using a secret the captain had told them, they picked their way through the area of poisonous snakes. At last they reached the castle, and the king banged on the door with the thunderbolt knocker.

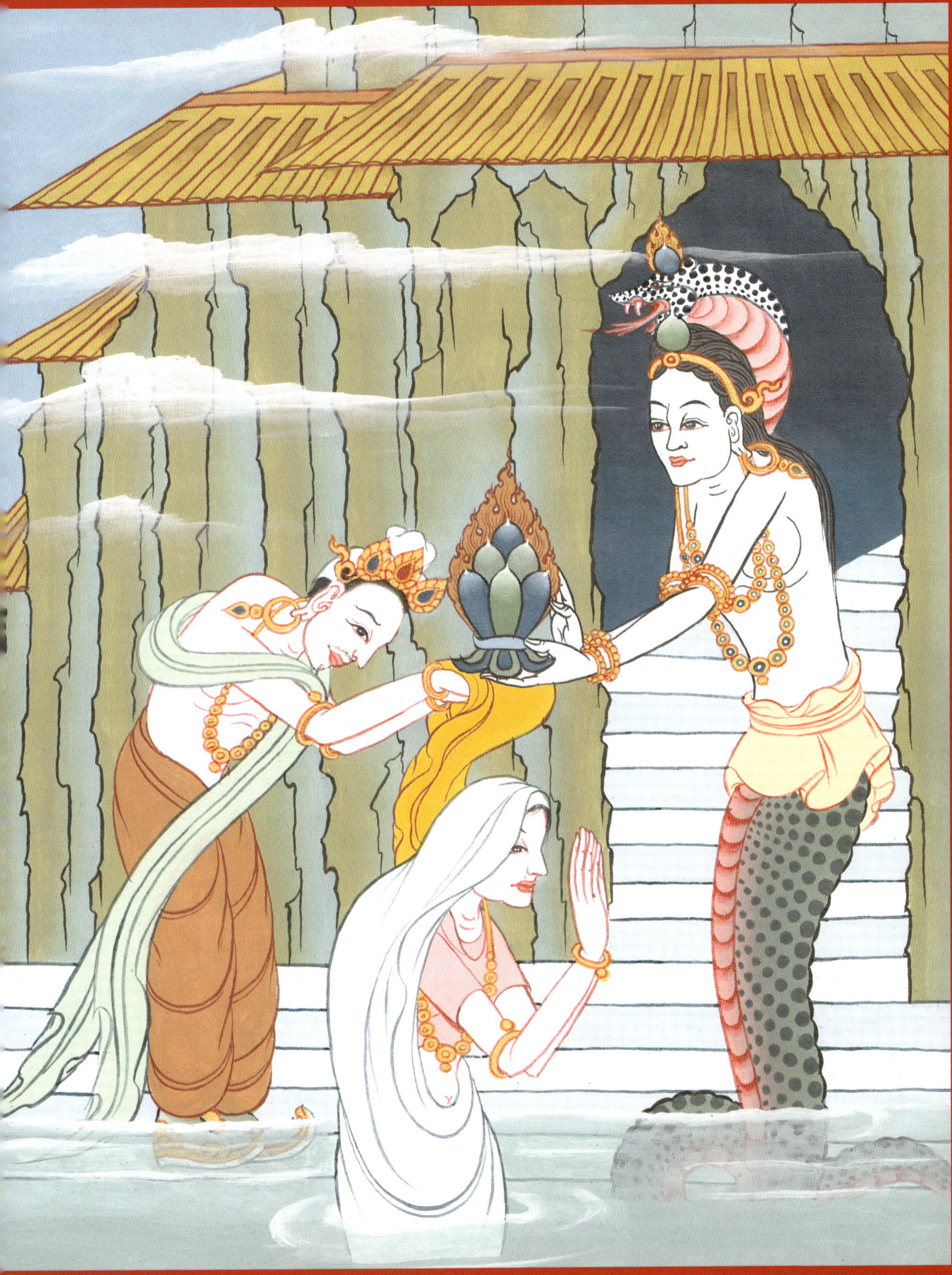

There was a great rumble, and the walls of the castle trembled. In a moment, the door opened and there stood a beautiful blue maiden, wearing a long gown of silk, many necklaces, and a crown set with a very large blue jewel. The jewel shone with the light of the five colors—white, blue, yellow, red, and green.

The princess greeted the king and queen and said in a melodious voice, "Ordinary people cannot reach the door of my house. It takes great courage. You must be very special people, and you must want something very much. What is it you have come for?"

The king and queen told the naga princess their whole story, and very humbly asked her to give them the Wish-Fulfilling Gem so they could feed their poor subjects. Their request filled the princess with joy, because helping people in need was just what the Wish-Fulfilling Gem was for. Without any hesitation, she took the great jewel from her crown and gave it to them.

"Here, Your Majesties," she said, "this is the great Wish-Fulfilling Gem that I received from my father, the king of the nagas. May it bring you and your kingdom wealth and happiness. Be sure to use it for the good of others."

The king and queen bowed, thanked the princess, and said goodbye. Then, holding the shining jewel, they wished themselves back to their ship and immediately arrived there. Once on the ship, they thought they would have no need to make a long voyage back to their kingdom. They expected that if they made a wish on the jewel, they would arrive home instantly. But to their surprise, their wish carried them to the shores of another island in the great ocean, which they did not recognize. They had no idea what it could mean that their wish had brought them to this place. They left their big ship and went ashore in a small boat to see what might be there.

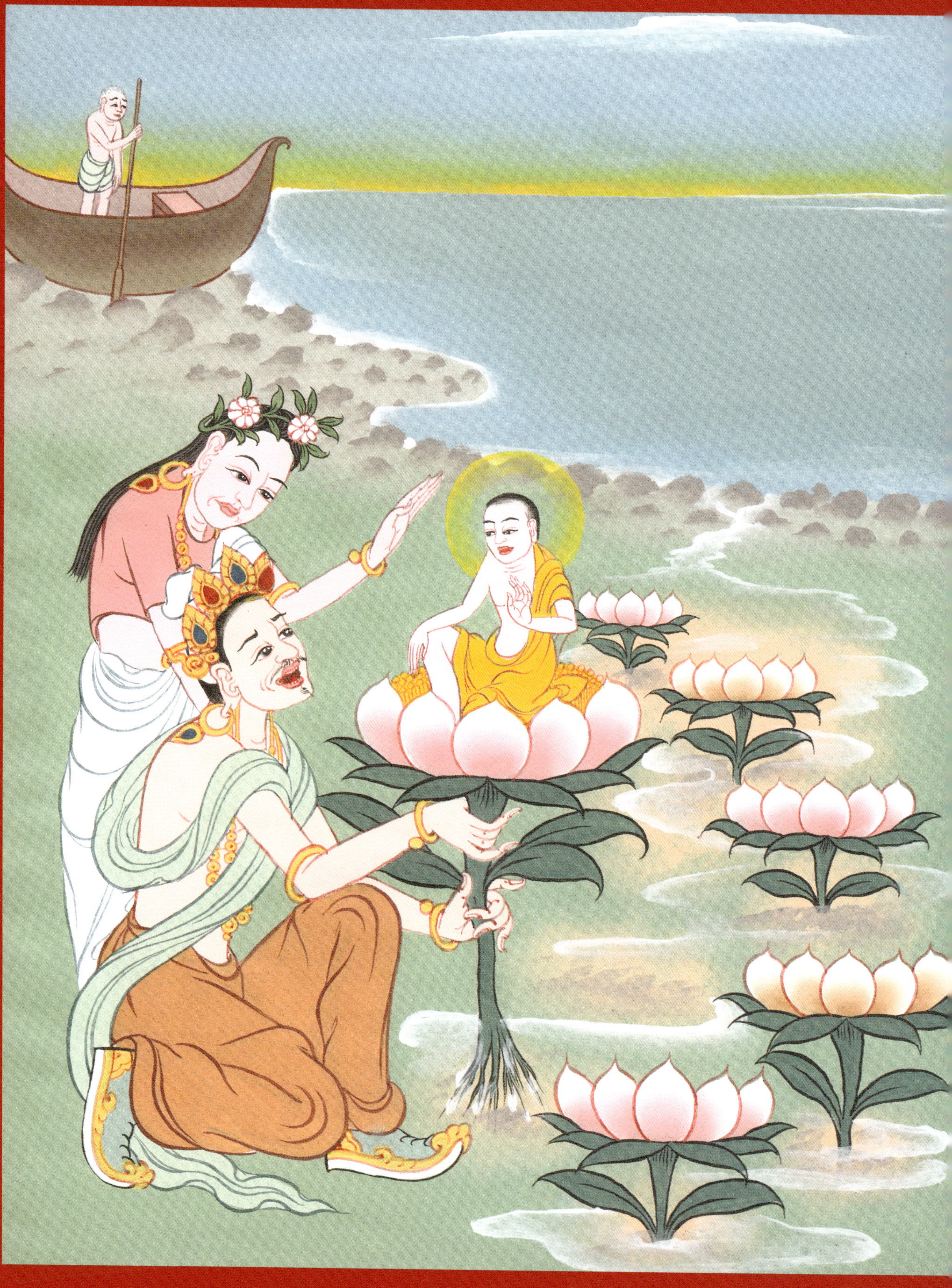

3

LOTUS-BORN

The king and queen pulled the boat ashore and began to explore. They hadn't walked far when they came to a beautiful lake with many colorful and sweet-sounding birds. In shallow water, growing out of the mud below, they saw a huge white lotus flower. Holding up their long robes in order not to get them wet and dirty, they waded out to inspect this amazing flower growing purely and spotlessly out of the mud. When they got close, they saw that in the middle of the flower there sat a beautiful young boy, radiant and smiling, with a wonderful knowing look in his eyes. He appeared to be about eight years old.

How could this be? they thought. *How miraculous!*

"Who are you? How did you come to be here?" the king asked the boy.

"Who are your father and mother?" the queen asked.

At first the boy was silent and just sat there smiling. The king and queen wondered whether he could talk at all. But at last he said, "I have no father and mother. I have just been born here."

"How wonderful!" said the king. "It would bring us great joy to be your mother and father."

"You are the child we have always wanted but never had," said the queen. "Will you be the prince, the heir to our kingdom?"

The little boy born from the lotus smiled in consent.

The king and queen were so happy they hugged each other and danced. The Wish-Fulfilling Gem had brought them a son as well as riches! They took the beautiful boy back to their ship, and again wished on the gem. This time their wish instantly brought them to the harbor of Odiyana. They could see their palace shining in the sunlight on the hill above, and the shores were lined with their cheering subjects, who were very happy that their king and queen had returned.

The next day, the king and queen called all their ministers, courtiers, and advisors together in the great palace hall. They had the Wish-Fulfilling Gem bathed in pure water so that it shone very brightly. As they carefully washed it with their own hands, their treasury slowly filled to the brim with gold, silver, and jewels. Their wish that nobody in the kingdom would be hungry or cold was fulfilled.

Then the king and queen had their new prince carried into the great hall on a cushion of silk. They announced, "This is our new son. We name him Prince Lotus-Born and proclaim him the heir to our kingdom."

Everyone cheered. The courtiers dressed the boy in royal robes, adorned him with jewels, and placed him on a high throne that rested on the backs of four stone lions. A princely crown was placed on his head. The royal musicians played, and songs of praise were sung. Everyone was happy because not only was the kingdom wealthy again but now it also had an heir. The great gem had fulfilled the king and queen's hidden wish.

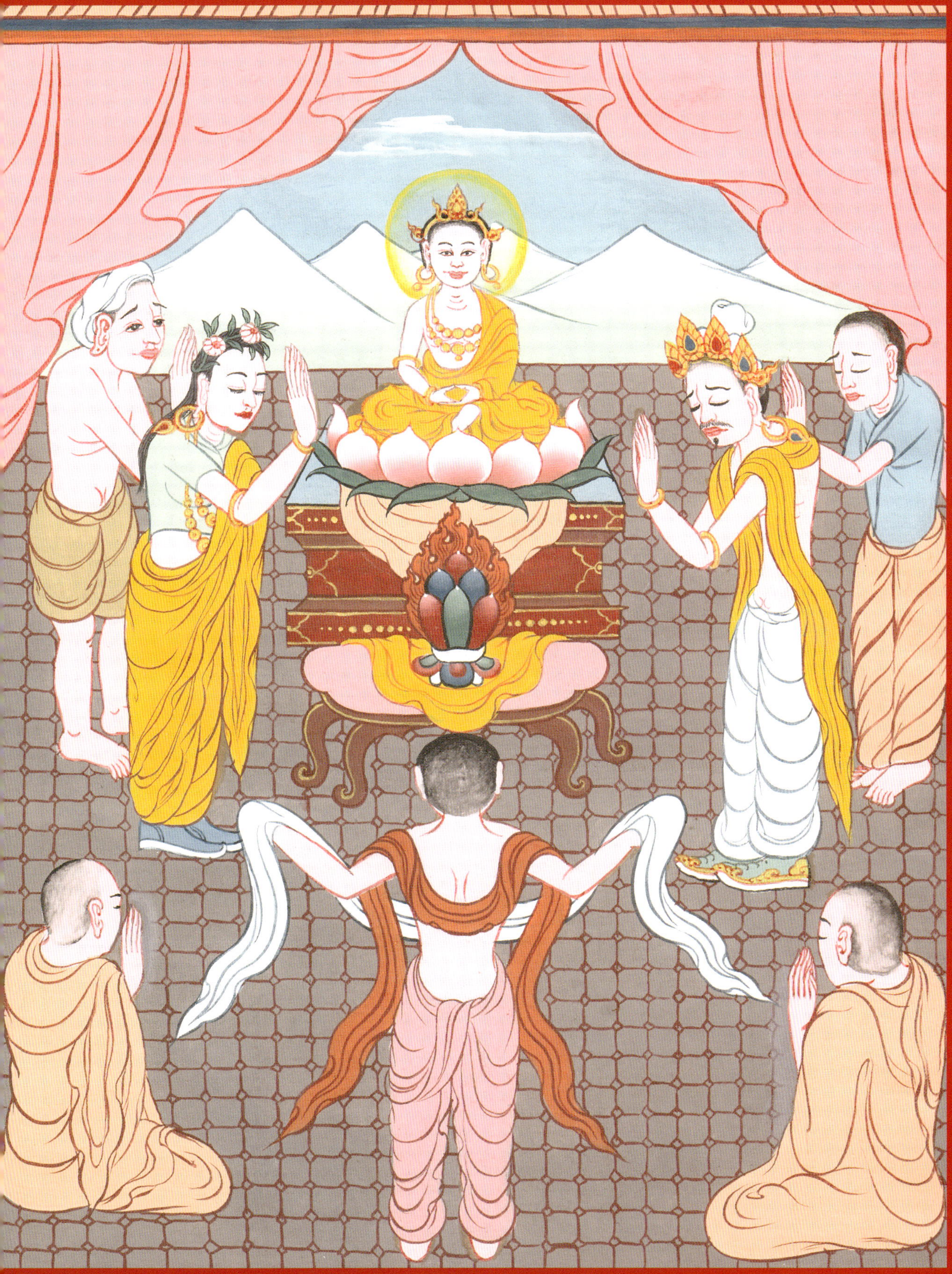

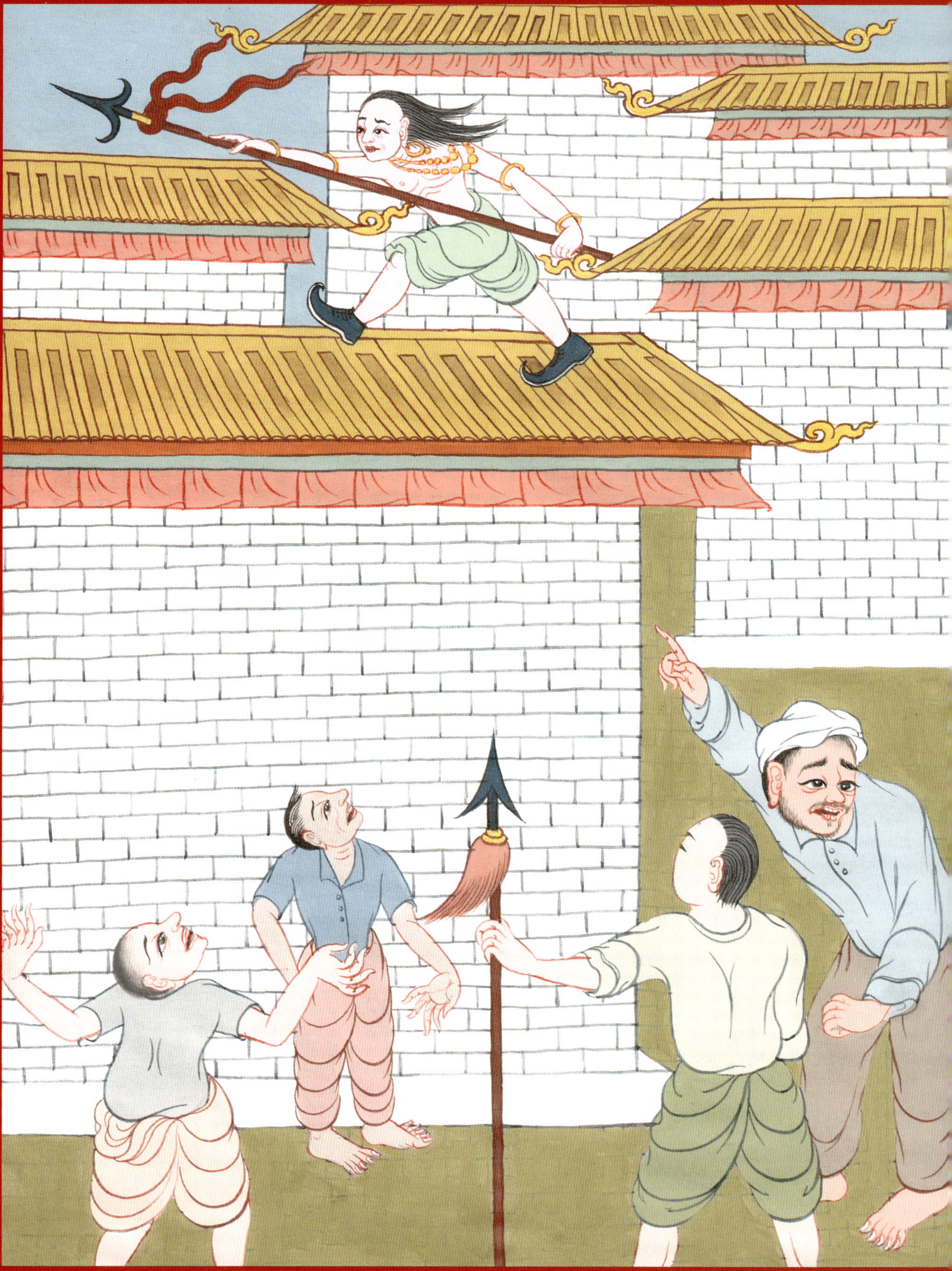

4

THE PRINCE'S MISHAP

Lotus-Born turned out to be a gifted child who learned things quickly. Everyone loved him, especially the king and queen. They gave him everything he wanted and even many other things that he didn't care about. At the same time, they were very strict with his training. Tutors taught the prince how to read and how to write, how to shape his letters with beauty and care. He was taught the history of his people, the martial arts, the science of plants and stars, and all the knowledge the royal advisors thought would prepare him to be a good king when it was time for him to rule.

By the time Prince Lotus-Born was a teenager, he was not so sure that ruling a kingdom was what he wanted. He had a feeling that other, more important things were waiting for him in his life. He was still loving toward his parents and all the people around him, but he began acting strangely. Sometimes he dressed like a wandering beggar and wasn't seen in the palace for several days.

One day, he was wearing strange clothes and dancing on the roof of the palace holding a scepter. A prince was not supposed to behave like this. And what is worse, he accidentally let the heavy scepter slip from his hand. It tumbled over the edge of the roof and landed far below on the head of the son of one of the king's courtiers, who was walking in the palace garden, killing him.

This was a great misfortune—a sad and terrible thing. The prince should never have been dancing on the roof, people said. The parents of the dead boy were filled with grief and anger. In fact, all the king's courtiers were furious at the prince's behavior. They demanded that the king punish the prince. The prince should be executed, buried alive, they said. But the king and queen loved the prince too much for this. They could not order his execution. Instead, Lotus-Born was exiled, cast out. He had to go far away. For twelve years he was not allowed to live in any house or town or anywhere among normal people. The only place he was allowed to live was in the charnel ground, the place where the bodies of dead people were burned or left to be eaten by animals. He had to smear his body with ashes and always carry a skull in his hand so that anyone who happened to see him would know that he had killed somebody.

This was supposed to be a terrible fate, but very strangely, when Lotus-Born was taken by the king's guards to the charnel ground and left there, he was not upset. He was not afraid to be alone. He was not afraid of death. Instead, he felt happy and free. Of course he missed his parents, whom he loved, but deep down he was glad not to be stuck anymore with the duty of ruling their kingdom. Alone among the corpses and wild animals, he felt strangely at ease. There were no courtiers and tutors to tell him what to do. In fact, there was nobody at all for whom he had to behave in any particular way. The dead could not tell anyone what to do. Lotus-Born had the feeling of a new life.

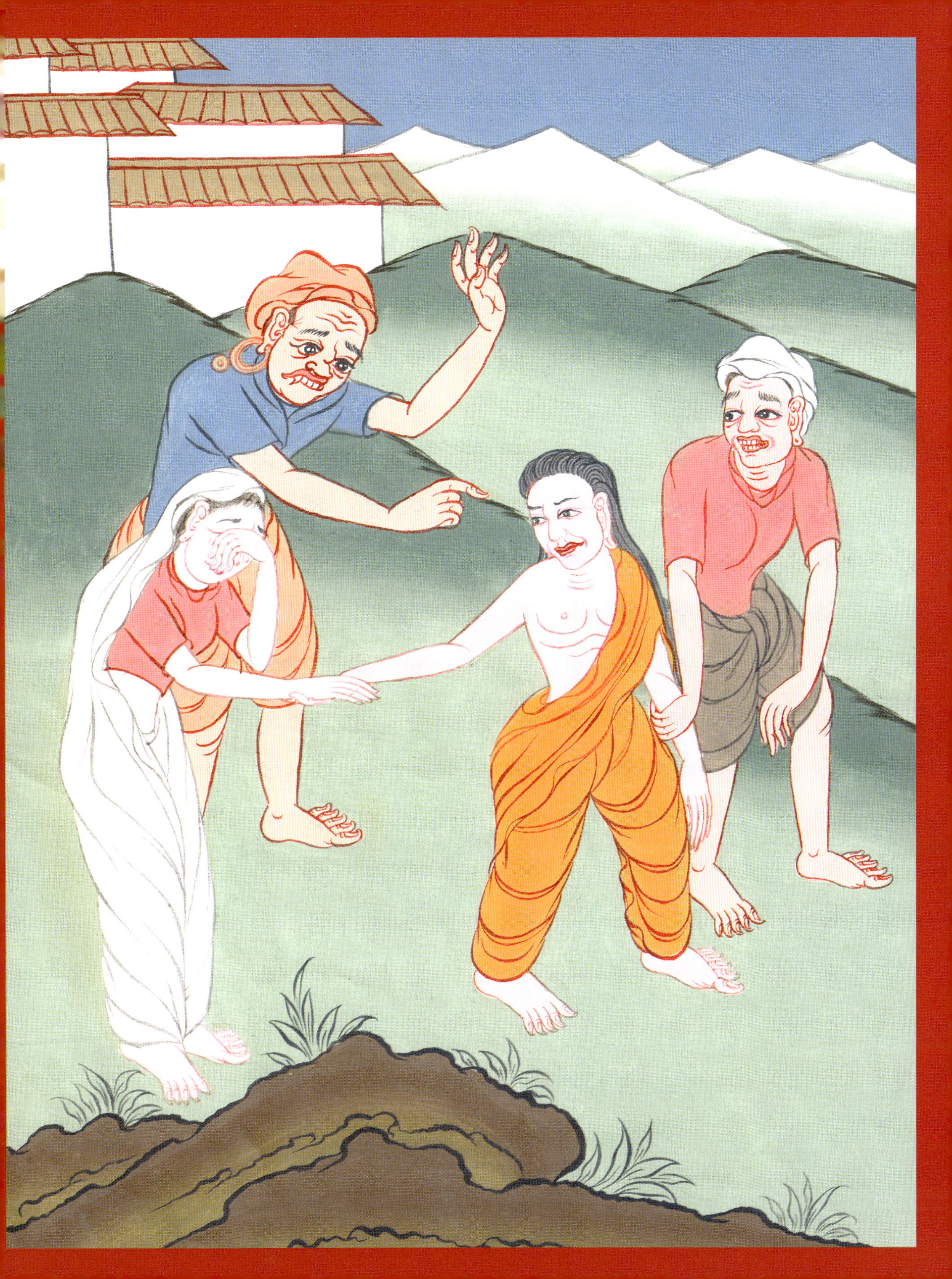

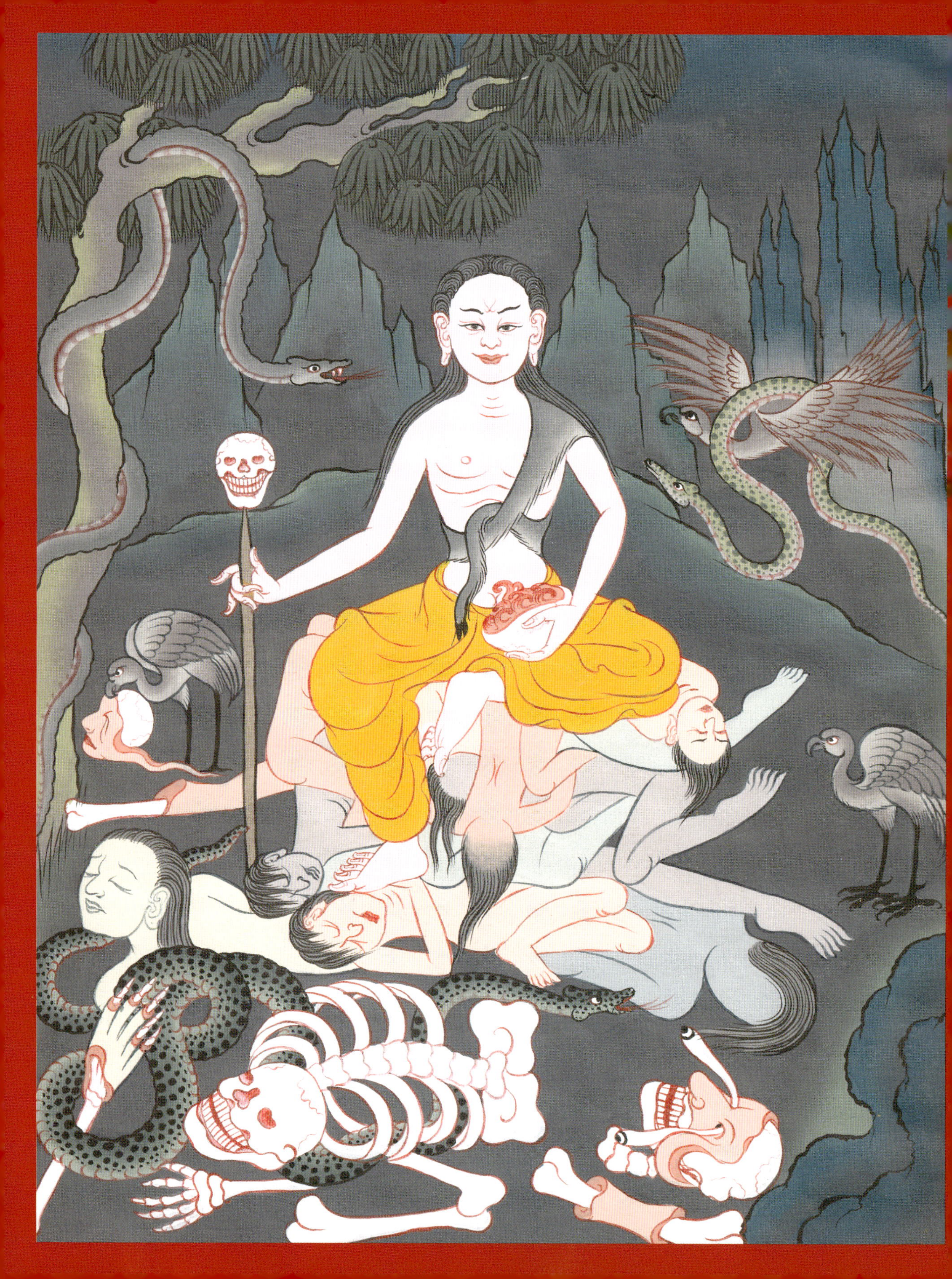

5

THE CHARNEL GROUND

Not long after arriving, Lotus-Born found that the charnel ground held not only the dead and the wild animals who fed on them, but it was also full of ghosts and spirits. The charnel ground was their world. Rarely did any living human stay there at night when the ghosts and spirits wailed and danced and fought with each other. But if the spirits ever did encounter a human at night, they appeared in their most terrifying forms, trying to frighten that person so badly that they would lose their mind. These ghosts and spirits fed on human life force, their source of power.

But Prince Lotus-Born had no fear of staying in the charnel ground at night. He simply lay down on the ground to sleep and covered himself with whatever rags he could find. The ghosts and spirits often came to frighten him. Sometimes just one came, and sometimes they came in a crowd. But to their surprise, Lotus-Born was never even a little bit afraid. The spirits' great fiery eyes and many arms that brandished skulls and weapons just made him giggle. After a while the spirits would go away feeling insulted, and the exiled prince would go back to sleep under his rags.

    The spirits became angrier and angrier, and one night, their queen came to confront Lotus-Born. She was a huge dark-red demoness with six arms and flames coming out of her body. She had long, sharp fangs, and in her many hands she carried spears, clubs, and other weapons. She approached Lotus-Born shrieking and wailing and hurling balls of poisonous yellow flames. Lotus-Born knew she had come to put an end to him, but he felt completely calm. Instead of running away, he got up and went straight toward the horrible demoness. He looked her straight in the eyes, which wasn't easy because she had three of them, and said, "O, Three-Eyes, you're so beautiful, won't you come and be my friend? I'd like to know you better."

    He laughed and threw one of her balls of poison flame back at her. Then he held the fiery glance of her three eyes with his own gaze, and they fought each other with their eyes. But not for long—Lotus-Born was much stronger, and soon Three-Eyes lay on the ground, whimpering and begging for mercy. Lotus-Born stripped away her power and let her go with the promise that she would serve him from then on. Since she was the queen of the charnel-ground spirits, all of them became his subjects and served him. Lotus-Born thus became the king of the ghosts and spirits of the charnel ground, and their power was his.

    Lotus-Born moved from charnel ground to charnel ground, avoiding the world of humans. He felt tremendous power within himself. Everywhere he brought the fearsome ghosts and spirits under his control and became their master and king. They bowed down to him, served him, and obeyed his commands. The spirits and demons called him King Thunderbolt, because of his power.

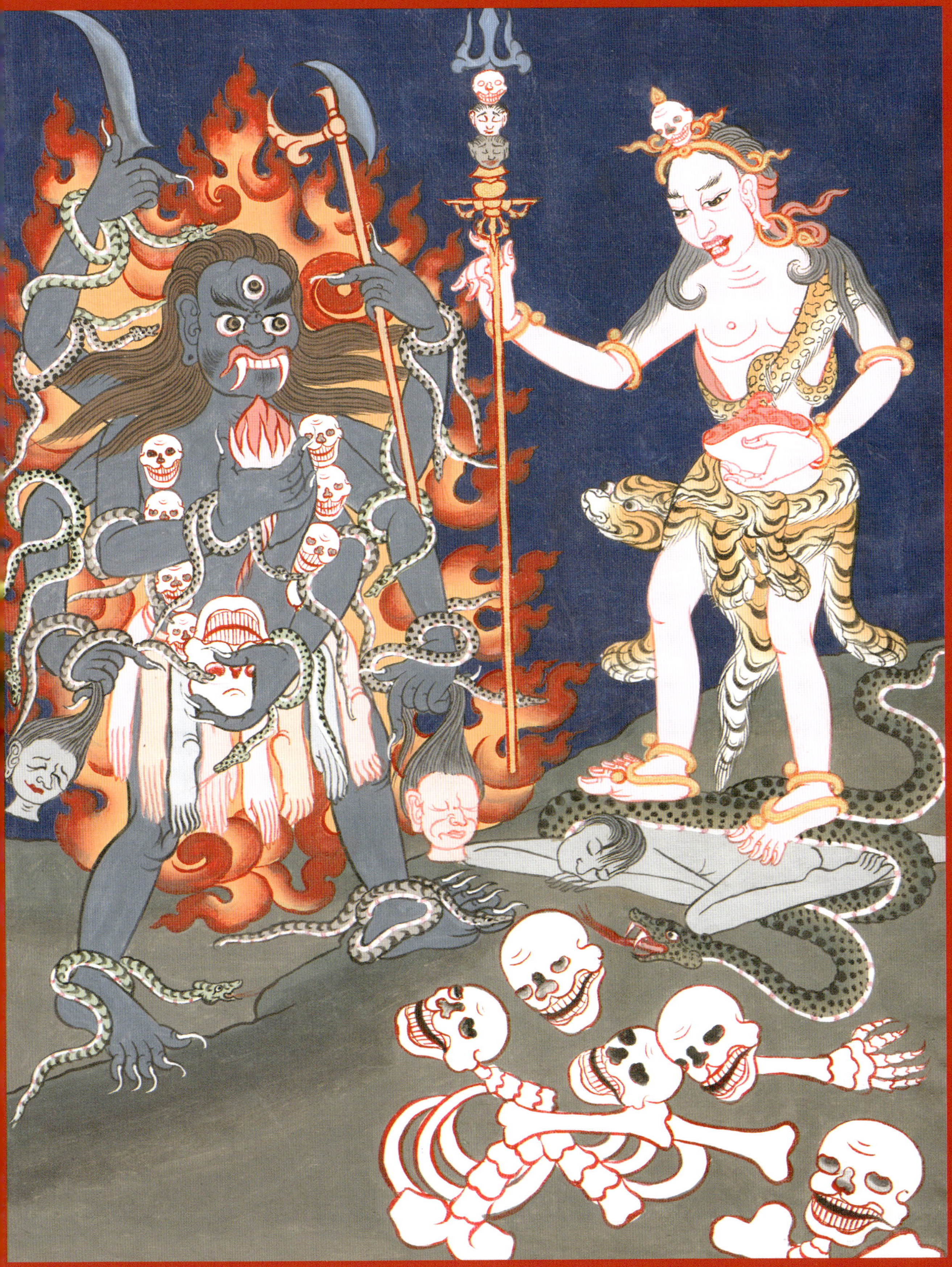

But despite all this power, soon Lotus-Born began to feel restless. He was glad he had escaped from ruling his parents' kingdom, but was ruling the demons any better? He looked around at his subjects. The one bowing in front of his throne just now was carrying her head under her arm. Others had three heads. Some of them were hanging upside down from tree limbs. In one way he was happy, because he had the very joyful feeling of knowing that he was not afraid of anything at all. He had conquered the charnel ground instead of being frightened by it. And he had learned much. He had learned how ghosts and demons wield their power with a kind of mental magic, and he had found that he had more power than they did. He was always stronger, because he knew that fear was not made out of anything real. So when he fought the spirits, he won easily, because fear was their main weapon. They used many tricks to frighten and overwhelm their victims, but Lotus-Born learned their tricks and outsmarted them. They were no threat to him. In fact, they were his servants. But was it really his destiny to be the king of ghosts and spirits? Sometimes he thought of the loving parents he had left behind and became very sad.

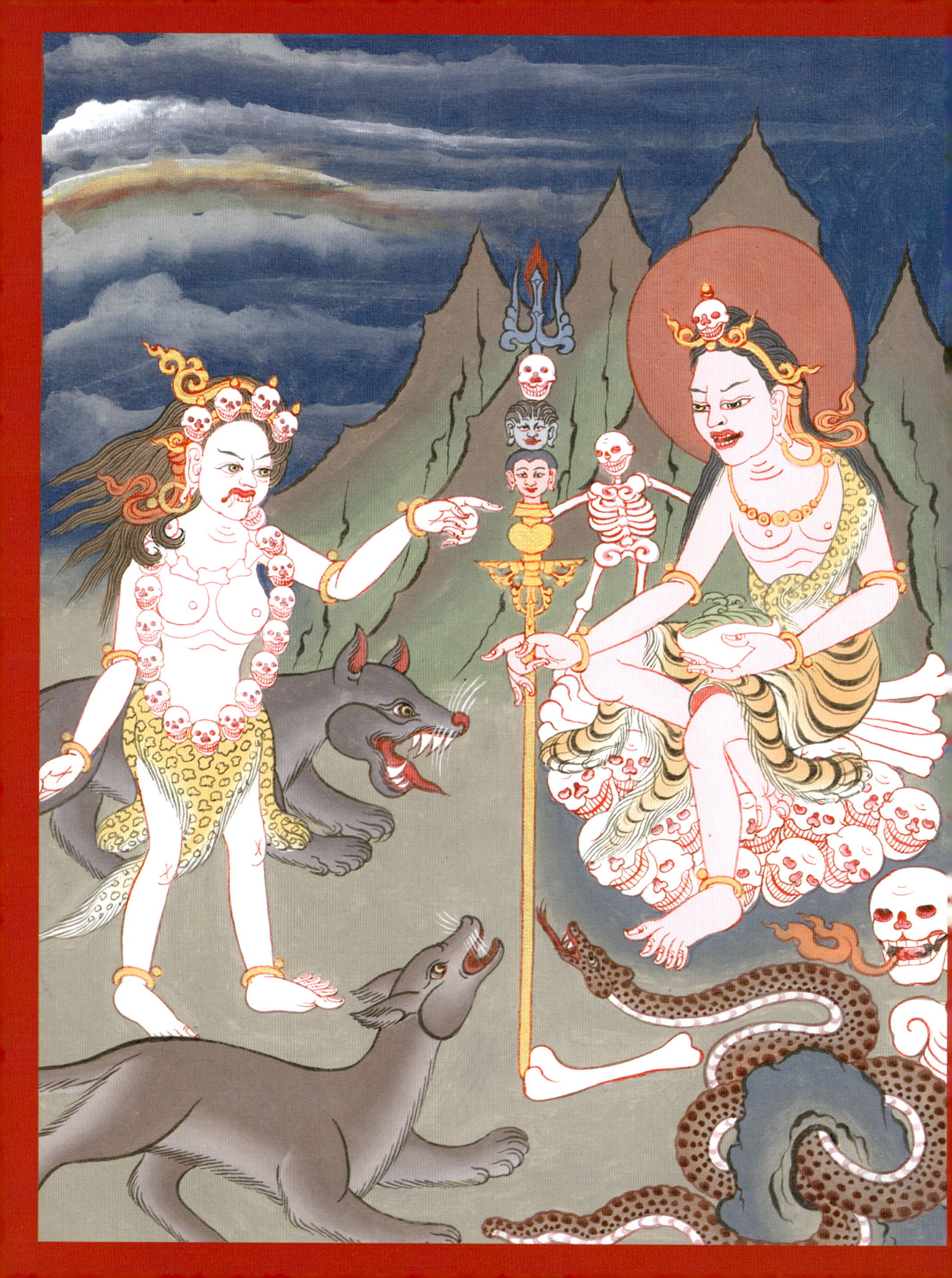

6

A DAKINI VISITS

One day, Lotus-Born was sitting in the charnel ground on his throne of bones, with a feeling of discontent. The moon had set, and the sun had not yet risen. It was neither night nor day. In a bare black tree not far in front of him, with jackals and wild dogs wandering around at the foot of it, he suddenly saw a red female spirit, a *dakini*, different from any kind of spirit he had seen before. She was beautiful. She was gazing at him calmly. She wasn't frightened of him the way the other spirits were. She was not in a hurry to please him the way the others were. She was smiling slightly, and her smile was lovely despite her small fangs. She wore a leopard-skin skirt and ornaments of bone and jewels. Lotus-Born was captivated by her smile. He couldn't take his eyes off her. Since she was so unlike the others, so composed and unafraid, he didn't know what to think or say, so he just sat there looking into her eyes, thinking nothing at all.

After a long time of looking at her this way, Lotus-Born had the feeling that he knew her. It was almost as though he had always known her, but he was rather sure they had never met.

At that moment the sun rose. It was morning, and the dakini spoke. "Who are you?" she said.

"Why, I'm King Thunderbolt, the king of the charnel ground," he said, shocked. "Don't you know?"

The dakini continued looking at him quietly for some time. Then she showed her fangs and said, "Who are you really? Have you forgotten?"

At first Lotus-Born was bewildered. What could the strange and beautiful dakini mean? All the beings in the charnel ground knew who he was—a wielder of great power, their lord and king! But then a memory glimmered in his mind, a memory from long, long ago, from before he had come to the charnel ground, from a time before he had even known his parents. To begin with, the memory was only a warm glow, but slowly an image came. He saw himself as a little child, sitting in the center of a large white flower, surrounded by wondrous rainbow light. In this vision there was a feeling of tremendous goodness that could never end. The child was fearless and powerful. This was how Lotus-Born also felt now. But remembering himself as the child in the flower made him feel this in a much bigger and deeper way.

When he looked back at the dakini, he saw that she, too, was surrounded by the soft but strong light of rainbows, many colors all coming together in a wonderful radiance. And now he saw, too, that the trees all around him were filled with beautiful dakinis, all bathed in that light.

These were the wisdom dakinis of the charnel ground, far different from the ordinary ghosts and spirits he had brought under his control. Until now they had not been visible to Lotus-Born. But now that he remembered who he truly was, he saw them clearly.

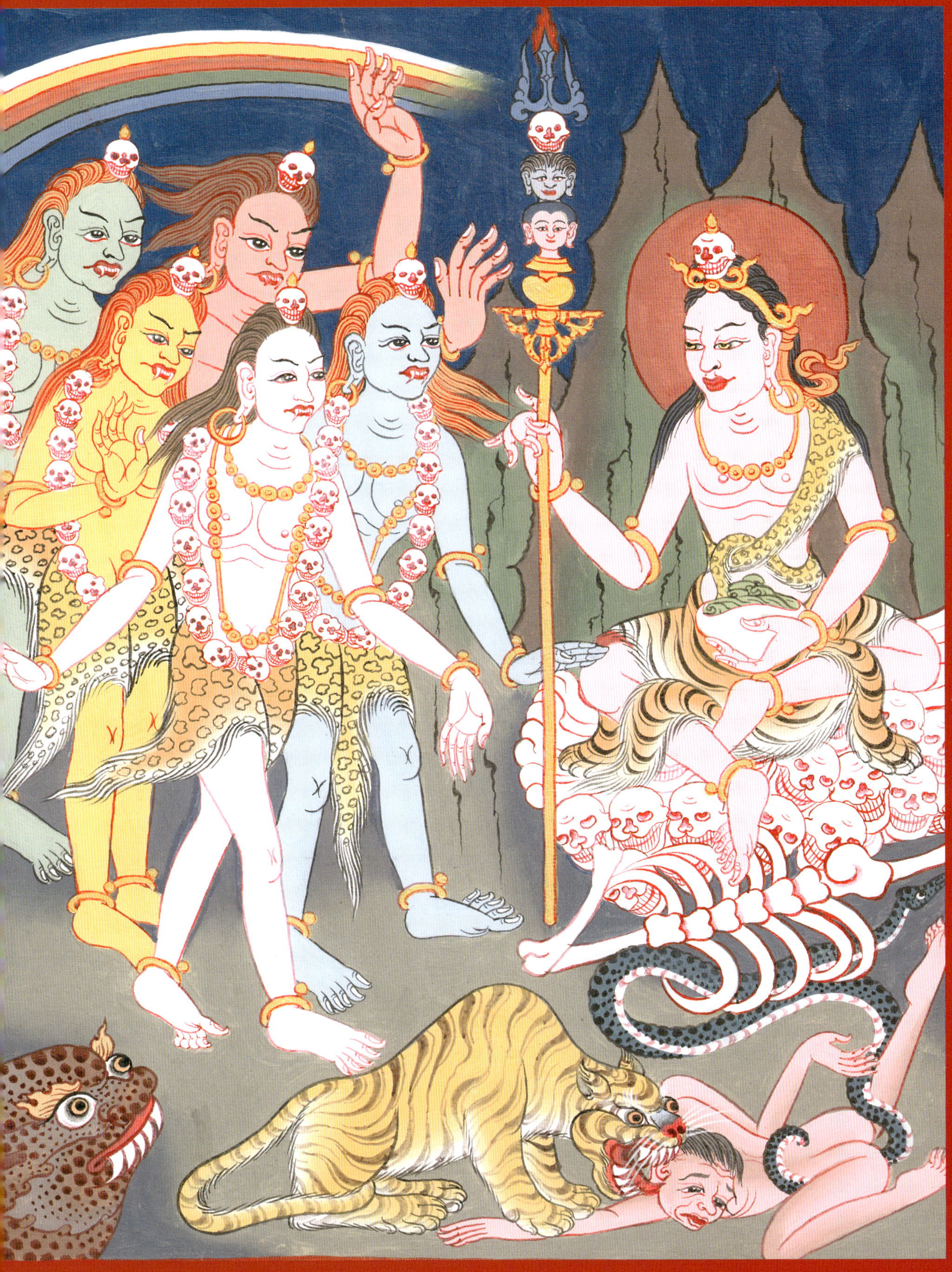

Some were red, some purple, some green, some blue, some yellow. Some of them had many arms—even six. But they were all very beautiful, and their gaze was full of love, kindness, and deep understanding. The ordinary ghosts and demons of the charnel ground could not see the wisdom dakinis, but some could feel they were there, and they hated and feared them. Now Lotus-Born saw the wisdom dakinis clearly. It was hard for him to believe he had lived here so long without seeing them, but he suspected they were one reason he had always felt at home in this supposedly horrible place.

From that point forward, the wisdom dakinis became his closest friends, loving friends like he'd never had before. Lotus-Born often sat together with them, and they taught him many things. One day, as he sat on the ground with them among the corpses, their leader told Lotus-Born some very important things that shaped the rest of his life.

"You are not just a king of ghosts and spirits. You are a buddha," she said. "I will explain to you what that is. *Buddha* means 'Awakened One.' As you remembered, you were born as a child of the heavenly buddhas. Now you are a human buddha and like the Awakened One, Gautama the Buddha, before you. You are the successor of that great teacher. You have to continue his work of waking people up."

"What do they have to wake up from, you may ask?" the wisdom dakini continued. "From hope and fear, the big causes of unnecessary suffering. Hopes that things are going to be the way they want, and fears that they won't be. Hoping and fearing instead of seeing things the way they are is like being asleep or like just being stuck all the time. In this state, people make up things that don't really exist and then worry about them. They are constantly getting excited and happy and disappointed and afraid about things that are not really happening. The job of a buddha is to wake them up from all that, so they can see things as they really are and realize their full potential."

"Deep down, you know all this already, Lotus-Born," said the wisdom dakini. "Especially now that we have met and talked, and you have remembered who you really are. You were awake from the beginning. That's why you were always fearless and never got caught up in the bad dreams of the charnel ground."

"But now the time has come for you to go to work. Do as Gautama the Buddha did: wake people up and relieve their suffering."

There was a pause. Then the wisdom dakini spoke again, with one of her special smiles.

"Don't you think your time has come, my dear child?" she asked.

"You're right, my lady," said Lotus-Born. "I always knew this was coming. But you have made it clear to me."

"That is so," said the wisdom dakini.

"I will always be grateful to you," said Lotus-Born, "and I will do my best to be a real buddha." He bowed to her and kissed her hand.

"That is good," said the wisdom dakini. "No matter what happens, our minds will never be separate."

She looked at Lotus-Born thoughtfully for a moment.

"You know," she said, "Gautama the Buddha was just like you. I remember him very clearly. He was also a prince who had to leave his home because he thought he had more important things to do than be a king."

Then with yet another loving smile, she blessed Lotus-Born and sent him on his way into the great world to help others.

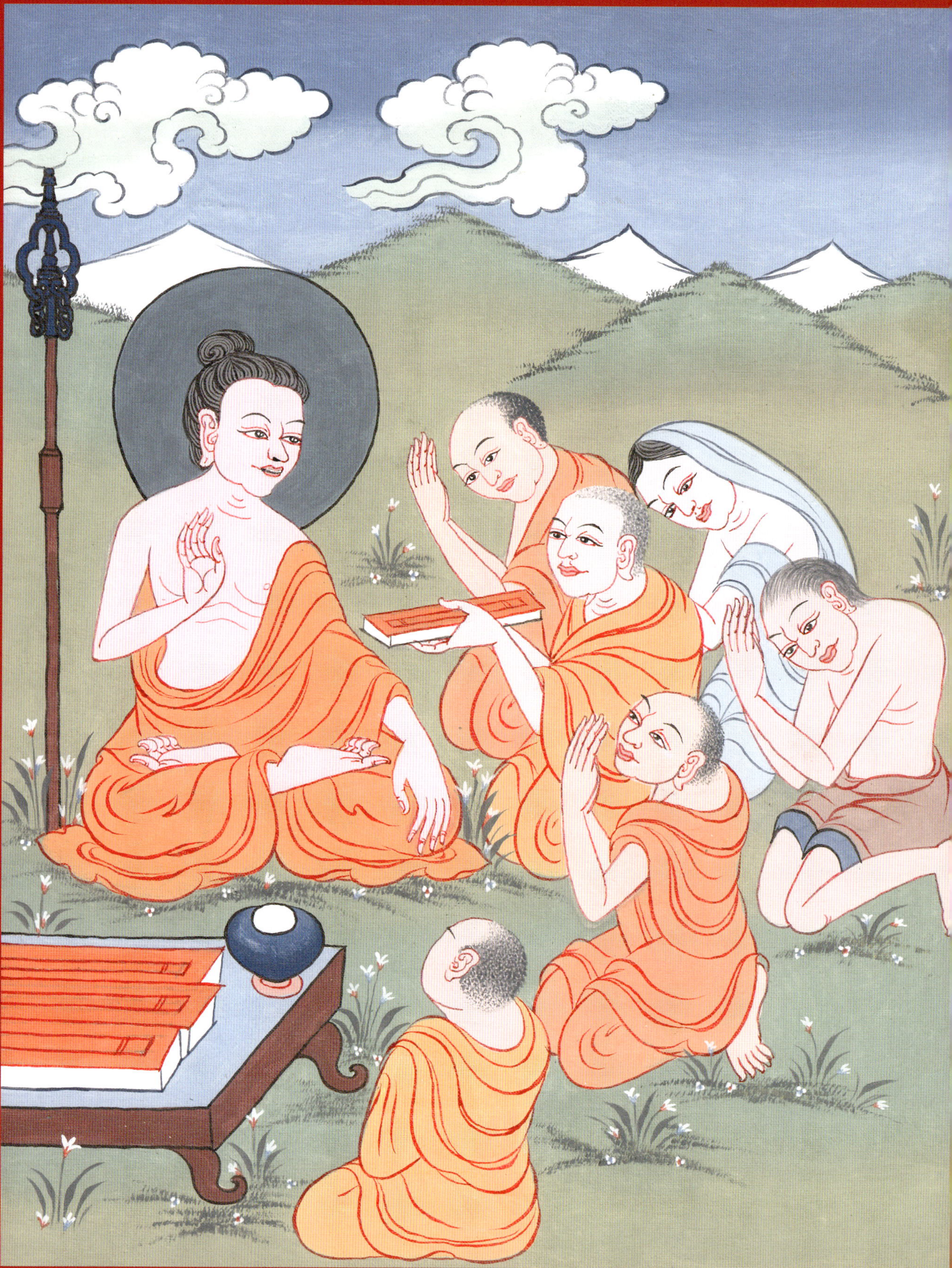

7

BACK IN THE WORLD OF THE LIVING

Lotus-Born left behind the realm of the dead and ghosts and demons and went out among ordinary people for the first time in many years. He was shocked to find how asleep most people were. They were living in their dreams, not recognizing what is real.

At the same time, Lotus-Born was a big shock to the people he met. He was dressed in rags he had picked off the bodies of corpses. He was dirty, and his hair was long, wild, and all knotted up from never being combed. He was not used to talking and shaping his face into the expressions that people are used to, such as smiles and frowns. Sometimes, without even thinking about it, he did things like flying from one place to another when he was in a hurry. This would have been normal in the world of spirits, but it was very frightening for ordinary people. Even when Lotus-Born didn't do magical or unusual things, often when people saw him, they screamed and ran away, thinking that he was a demon. Even though he had the wisdom of wakefulness, he didn't know how to behave skillfully in the ordinary world. All he wanted to do was help people, but instead he was having the opposite effect.

He decided to find the followers of Gautama the Buddha and learn how they help people wake up from their imaginary hopes and fears. Along the way, a kindly old couple took Lotus-Born in, let him take a bath, and gave him some ordinary clothes. Now he no longer looked frightening—in fact, he was a very handsome young man. He also learned to not do things that would scare people. So he would only fly at night, when nobody could see it.

Soon Lotus-Born found some followers of the Buddha and began to study with them. He decided that it would be beneficial to adopt these teachers' methods of training and attire for a time. Lotus-Born learned that a person who was doing the work of trying to wake people up was called a *bodhisattva*, which means "wakefulness person." He learned that bodhisattvas teach people simple things such as generosity and patience. They also show people how to do both sitting and action meditation, which teaches them to not get caught up in their dreams and to stay present; when they fall back into their imaginations and begin wandering around in them again, they must meditate some more.

Lotus-Born studied with many Buddhist teachers and read all their books about how to wake people up. Of course, he understood everything immediately, because he was already awake himself. He realized that the whole waking-up thing was simple, just like a snap of the fingers, but long books had to be written about it because people's minds kept wandering and they had to be reminded of the same thing over and over again in different ways. Lotus-Born understood that sometimes people need a lot of support and encouragement to see through their dreams, which they are often quite attached to. Because he understood all this so well, he received the blessings of many Buddhist teachers, and it was not long before he himself became a famous Buddhist teacher.

Soon, just as before when he was a prince in his parents' palace and again when he was the king of the charnel ground, Lotus-Born realized that he was not yet doing enough to help suffering beings. But this time he understood very well what he had to do, and he had a much better idea of how to do it. If people could learn the skill and wisdom of meditation, they had a good chance of being freed from their fear of being alone, their fear of death, and other imaginary worries.

At that time, a very unexpected thing happened to him. He fell in love. He was traveling in the kingdom of Zahor in northern India, which also happened to be the first place he had gone after leaving the charnel ground. The first time he was there, he was a scary wild man people thought was a demon. Now he was considered an important person, and he was invited to visit the king's palace. There he met Princess Mandarava, the king's favorite daughter. Lotus-Born and Princess Mandarava fell in love the moment they saw each other. Although the princess was closely guarded, one night she was able to slip away from the palace and meet Lotus-Born. The two ran away together and hid in a cave outside the city.

To Lotus-Born, Mandarava was like a wisdom dakini in human form, which in this case was the form of a very beautiful young woman. Mandarava saw Lotus-Born as the wise and handsome prince she had always been waiting for. They decided to stay together and live in the cave. Lotus-Born taught Mandarava the wisdom of the Buddhadharma (teachings of Buddhism), and they meditated together. Soon she reached the state in which she was free from hope and fear, and they were both equally awake like buddhas.

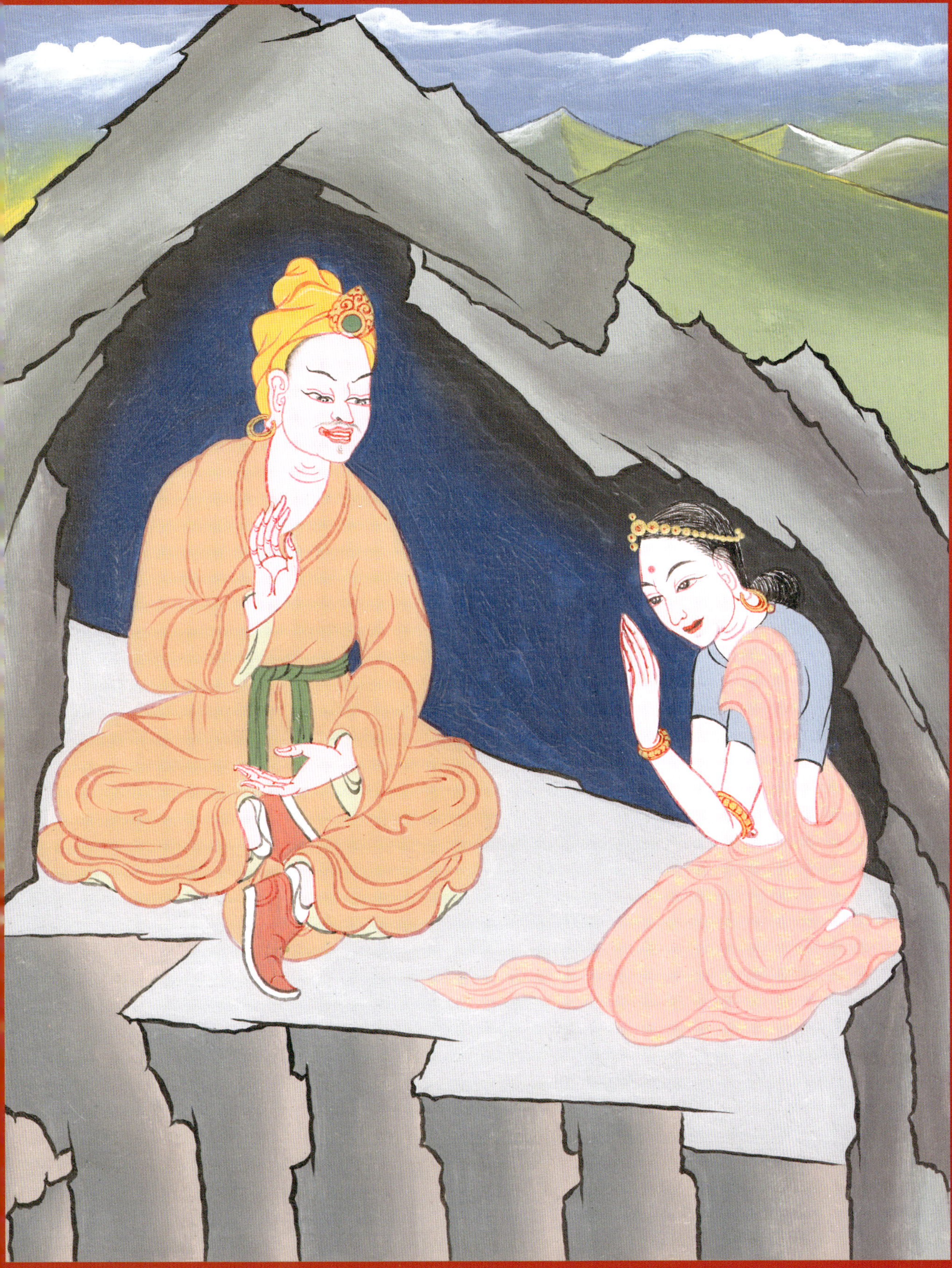

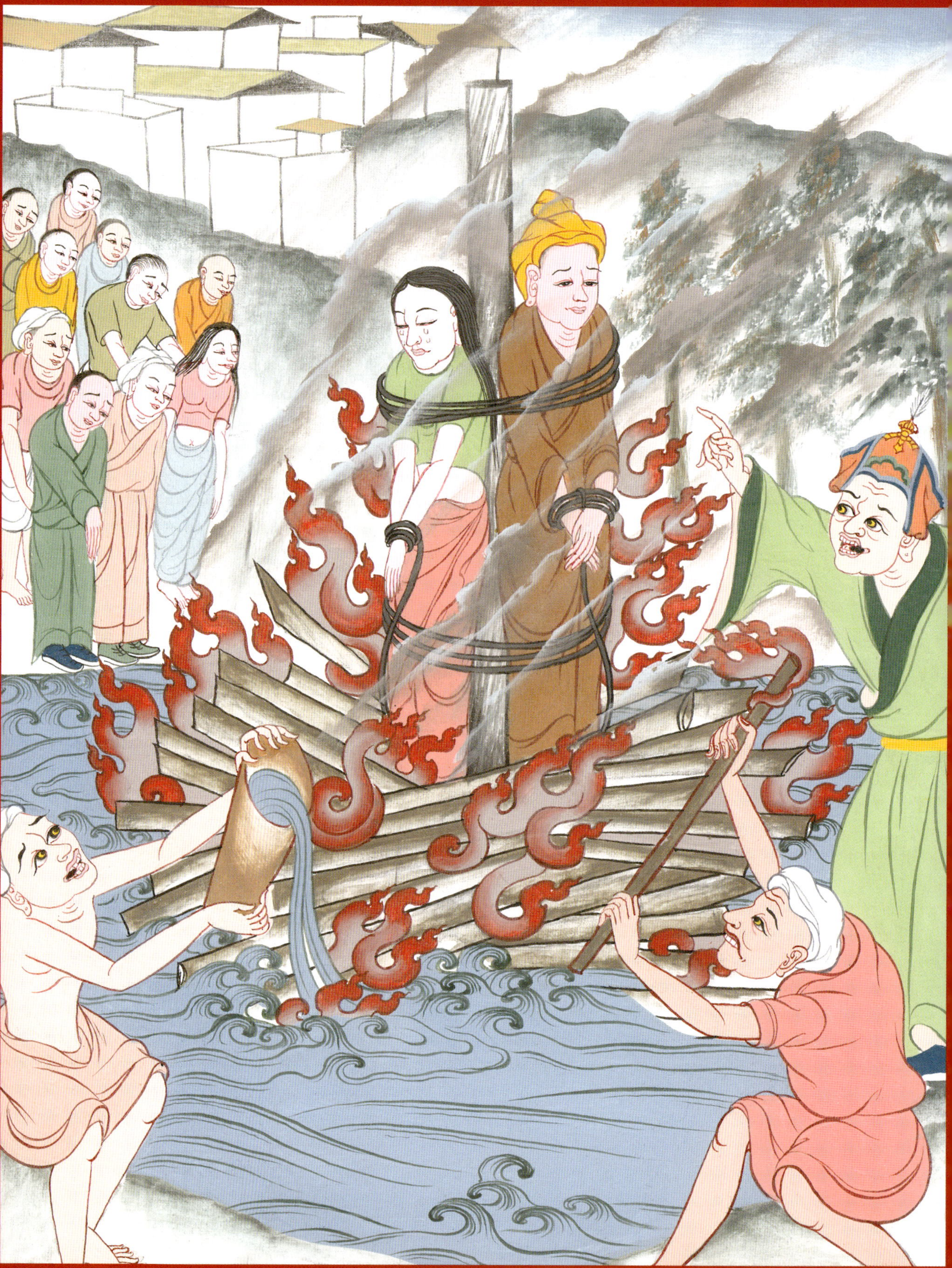

8

THE LAKE OF FIRE

Lotus-Born and Mandarava decided to go back to the city and teach the Buddhadharma so they could share love and happiness with everyone. But when people saw them, instead of welcoming them, they were angry at Lotus-Born because he had stolen their princess. And they were angry at the princess because she had run away and brought shame on the kingdom. Then someone recognized Lotus-Born as the wild man who had been there before. A crowd gathered.

"Our princess has run away with a demon!" they shouted. The crowd got very excited. Everyone was yelling as loud as they could, and some were waving weapons.

"They must be punished!" a woman screamed.

"They must be punished," the crowd echoed.

"We'll burn them alive!" the woman shouted.

"Burn them, burn them!" the crowd shouted. "Burn them right now!"

A few of the people grabbed Lotus-Born and Mandarava and carried them off to a square in the center of the city, near the palace. The others gathered huge piles of wood and big jars of oil.

The king and queen learned what was happening. They had been looking all over for their daughter. Now they, too, were furious to learn that their daughter had run off with a demon.

"They must be burned," said the king.

"Let the people burn them!" said the queen.

Lotus-Born and Mandarava were tied to a stake in the middle of a huge pile of wood. Oil was poured on the wood and it was lit. The flames roared up and soon they were so high that Lotus-Born and Mandarava, who remained completely calm the whole time, could no longer be seen behind them.

After nine days, the wood pile was still smoking. Usually when criminals were burned, the fire and smoke died out after three days. But the wood pile prepared for Lotus-Born and Mandarava was still smoking after nine days. This made people curious, and when they came to see what was happening, the fire blazed up again and began to spread. The people saw that within the flames the oil had turned into a large lake. In the middle of the lake, on a huge open lotus flower, Lotus-Born and Mandarava sat together, fresh and cool, smiling and completely unharmed.

Meanwhile, the flames had begun to burn the palace and the rest of the town. The king and queen came running and a large crowd gathered. The king and queen managed to get through the flames and fell to their knees on the edge of the miraculous lake.

"O, Lotus-Born One," they called out, "we were so wrong not to recognize you as a buddha. Please have mercy, save us from the flames, and teach us."

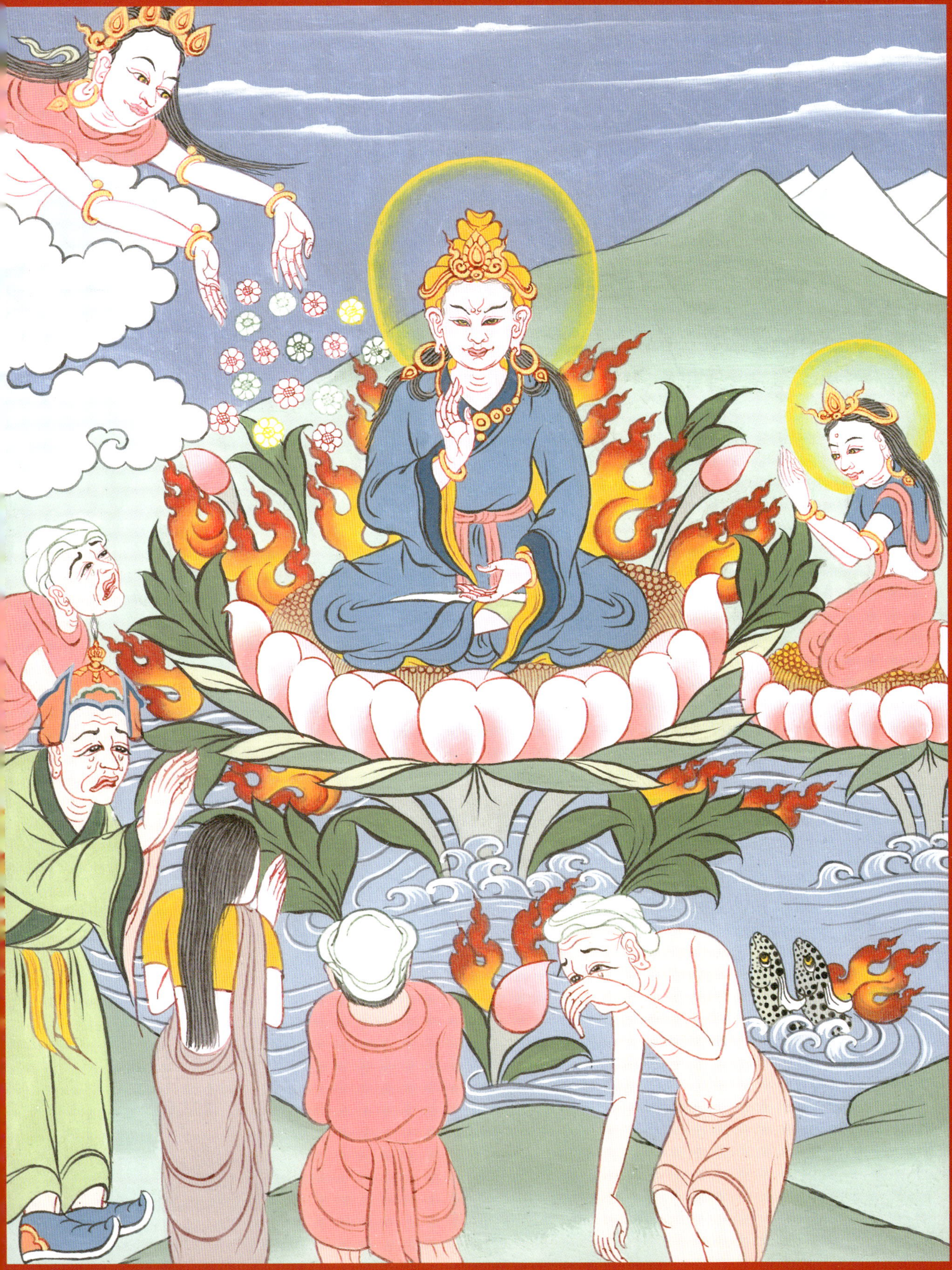

They begged and begged and bowed down again and again. Gradually the fire died down and the town was saved. The lake disappeared, and Lotus-Born and Mandarava stood among the people. Everyone fell to their knees along with the king and queen and praised Lotus-Born as the miraculous being he was, and they praised their own Princess Mandarava, who was now part of the miracle. They promised to try to wake up, beginning by doing no harm to other people and being kind and generous to one another.

Lotus-Born now felt that he was doing what he was supposed to do with his life. His time with Mandarava had shown him the way to sharing his happiness and wisdom with others. Lotus-Born had learned that loving one person very much is very close to loving everybody. The best way he knew to share his love was to spread the teachings of the Buddha and help as many people as possible to wake up from their suffering. Lotus-Born decided to part ways with the people of Zahor to meditate in the charnel ground to further his understanding.

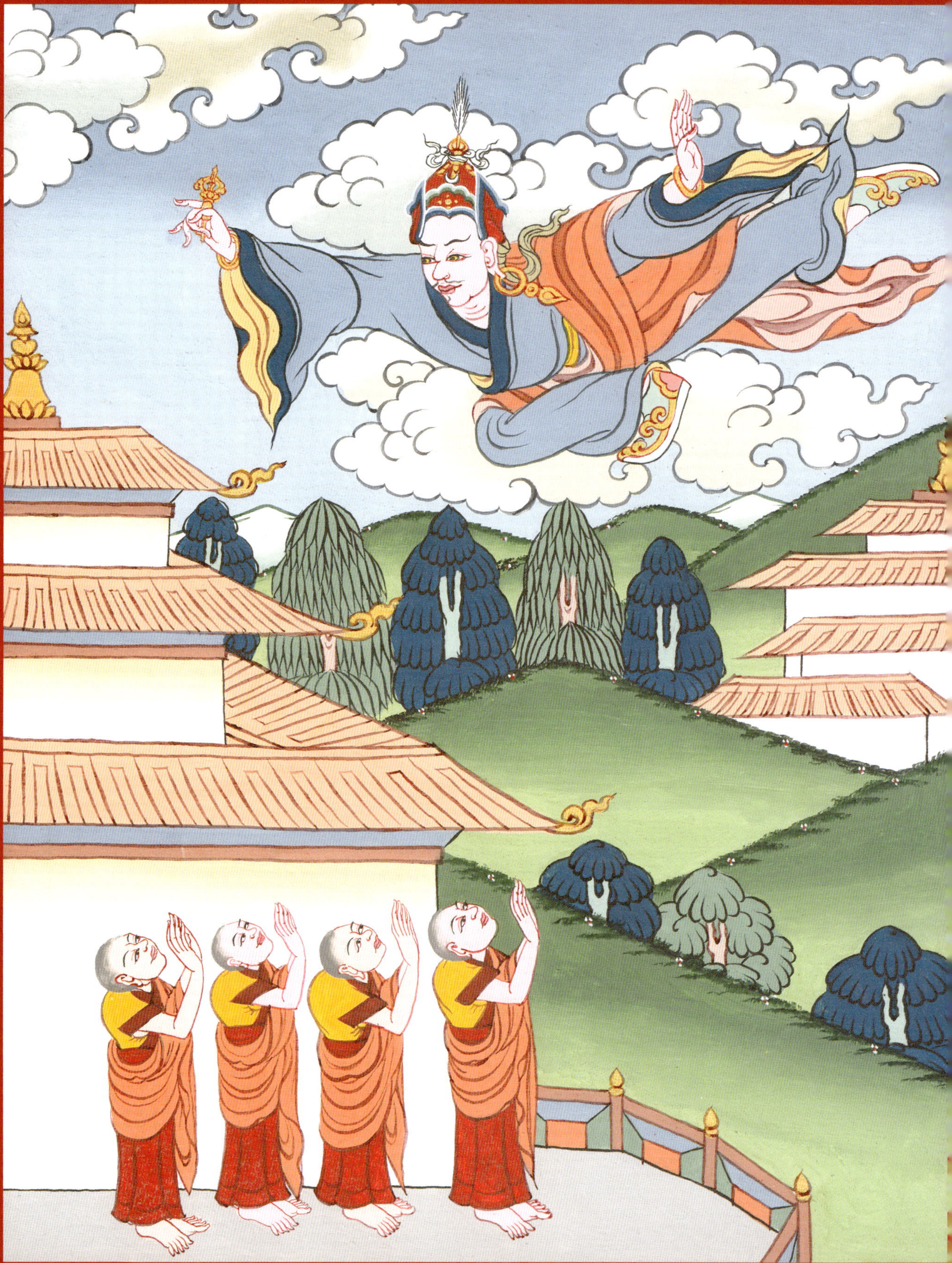

9

THE GREAT DEBATE

At Vajra Seat, a place of great importance to the Buddhists, where Gautama the Buddha had meditated, a huge struggle was taking place. Four evil and powerful magicians with their hundreds of followers were challenging the Buddhist teachers. There was to be a great contest, first in debate and then in sorcery and magic. The two sides had agreed that if the magicians won, the Buddhist teachers as well as all the people in the country were to give up the teachings of the Buddha and become the subjects of the magicians. If the Buddhists defeated the magicians, everyone was to accept the Buddhist teachings.

The Buddhist teachers at Vajra Seat had no trouble defeating the magicians in argument and logic. But the contest in magic and sorcery was still to come. The magicians were very powerful and knew many evil spells, and the Buddhists would likely be defeated and destroyed. In the night, the Buddhists held a council in a cave deep beneath their stronghold. They were desperate. They needed a plan, but they couldn't think of one that would work. They were getting ready to face defeat when something amazing happened.

A figure appeared in the air above their heads. At first they thought it was a trick of the flickering torchlight playing on the uneven rocky walls of the cave. But it was a blue-skinned woman carrying a broken stick—a wisdom dakini—hovering in the air.

"You are sure to be defeated by the evil magicians," she told them, holding up the broken stick, "unless my brother is here to help you."

"Who is your brother," one of the teachers asked, "and where is he?"

"He is called Lotus-Born. He is meditating in a charnel ground," said the dakini.

"How can we get him here to help us?" they respectfully asked her. "Please tell us what to do."

"There is no time to send a messenger," she said. "And besides, he is not anywhere where a messenger could find him. The only way to get him here is to call to him in your minds. I will give you the words to say."

She gave them an invocation to recite, and they all got down on their knees to pray for Lotus-Born to come.

HUM
In the northwest of the land of Uddiyana,
On a blooming lotus flower,
You have attained supreme, wondrous siddhi.
You are renowned as Padmakara,
Surrounded by your retinue of many dakinis.
We practice following your example.
Please approach and grant your blessing.
GURU-PADMA-SIDDHI HUM

Then they went to sleep holding Lotus-Born in their hearts.

In the morning when the teachers went outside to face the magicians, Lotus-Born arrived, flying through the sky, and landed in front of them like a bird. The four magicians arrived surrounded by hundreds of their followers. They shouted insults and threats and began hurling fireballs and casting spells. Black poisonous smoke came billowing toward Lotus-Born and the Buddhist teachers. Flashing flames flared in their faces. The Buddhist teachers thought that they were sure to be killed and their cause lost. But Lotus-Born took the form of a horrific demon wearing a necklace of skulls. He blew away the magicians' smoke and flames with a fierce wind from his mouth. He hurled huge, razor-sharp whirling wheels at them. He sent hailstorms, lightning, and a rain of hot coals they could do nothing to stop. With ease, Lotus-Born defeated and destroyed the magicians. When he was done, he waved his hand and what was left of them vanished entirely. Their terrified followers scattered in all directions. There was nothing left of the enemy. The battle was over. Vajra Seat was saved, and the Buddhist teachings could flourish throughout the country. Everyone praised Lotus-Born. Banners were raised, horns were blown, and a huge feast that lasted for many days was given in his honor.

Lotus-Born himself was very pleased with his victory. It seemed that his life was taking the direction it was meant to take, but he felt that his understanding was not yet complete. In order to fully realize the qualities necessary to save all the people of the world from suffering unnecessarily, he went to Great Rock Cave in the mountains of the north to meditate.

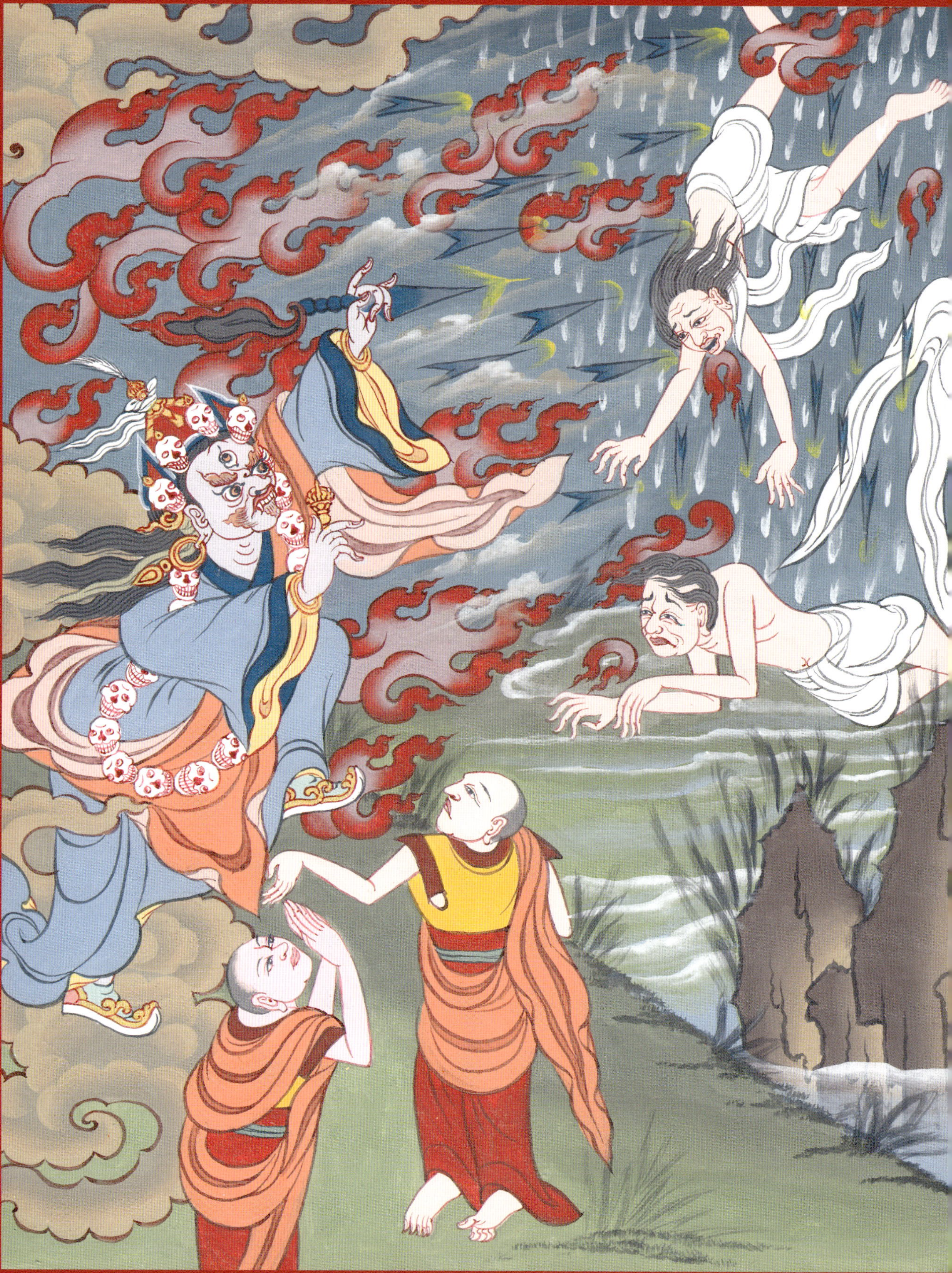

Lotus-Born did not leave Great Rock Cave for a long time, but through the power of his mind he traveled through different universes. He met many miraculous beings, some of them wonderful, some of them horrid. He battled demons in other worlds and forced them to stop making trouble in this world. His power and his wisdom grew and grew. Even though he was now very famous and many people, including kings and queens, wanted to see him, he chose to stay meditating in the cave where almost no one knew to find him.

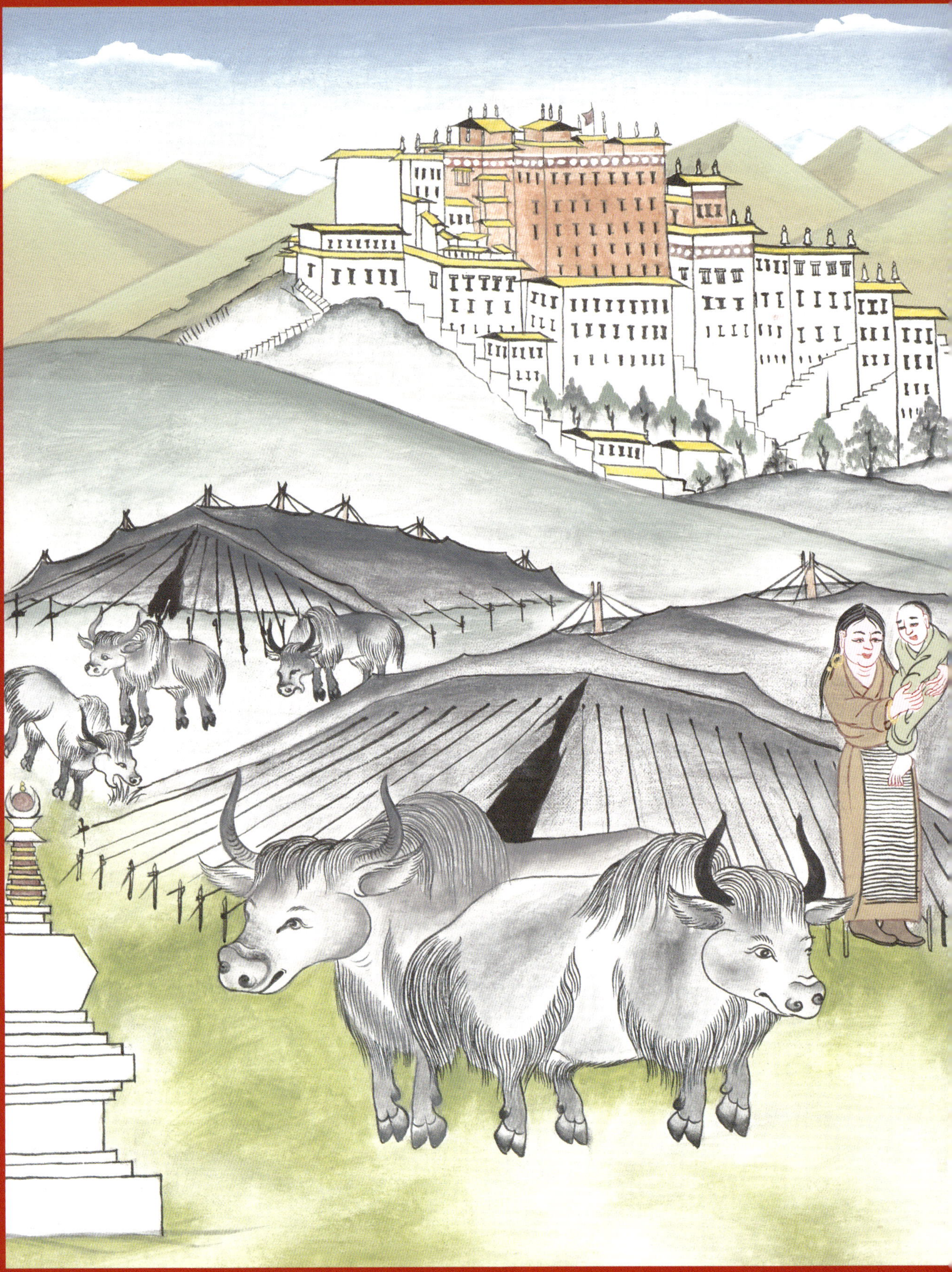

10

THE LAND OF SNOWS

Some years before Lotus-Born went to Great Rock Cave to meditate, a heavenly buddha named Manjushri was sitting on top of a five-peaked mountain, which was his home on earth. From this mountaintop, with his powerful mind and limitless vision, he was looking out to see what he could see.

The heavenly buddha Manjushri saw a big, beautiful country of high snowcapped mountains and many lakes, deep valleys with rivers running through them, and immense open plains. It was all very high up in the thin air, and the sunlight was extraordinarily strong and bright. In the early morning, the snow-covered mountaintops shone pink. In this place known as the Land of Snows, or Tibet, small groups of people, far away from one another, were living in tents. They herded yaks and other animals and frequently moved from place to place to find fresh grass for them. There were some towns, too. In the biggest town, Lhasa (Place of the Gods), the king and queen lived in their castle. But most of this big, beautiful country of mountains, rivers, canyons, and plateaus was empty and silent. The wind blew, rivers rushed, and rain fell. Sometimes a wolf howled. Sometimes a fox barked. Sometimes a rock, loosened by a snow lion's foot, clattered down a hillside. In the great silence, every little sound could be heard from near and far.

In the places where there were no people, there were many spirits living in the rocks and waters, in the air and under the ground. In fact, there were many more spirits in this land than there were people. Six sister spirits lived on a narrow mountain ledge. In a big pile of blue rocks lived nine demons who were brothers. In one place was a powerful mountain spirit who sometimes appeared as a white yak. In another place was a lake spirit who took the form of a beautiful woman. There were spirits of all forms; sometimes they were visible and sometimes not. Most people couldn't see them, though they knew they were there. Some people were more alert and could see them most of the time. The powerful, beautiful, and helpful spirits people called "gods," and the nasty, mean, ugly, and jealous spirits they called "demons." But most of the spirits were neither gods nor demons. All these spirits could be either friendly and helpful or unfriendly and mean, depending on whether they liked you or not.

The people of Tibet shared their hidden land with all these spirits. They tried to please the spirits by making offerings of food, drink, and fragrant smoke. They were not only busy with the spirits, but they also often fought with each other. They had family feuds, wars between neighbors, fights over who owned which valley and who took water from which spring. In fact, the people made the spirits uneasy and angry because they could not be at peace.

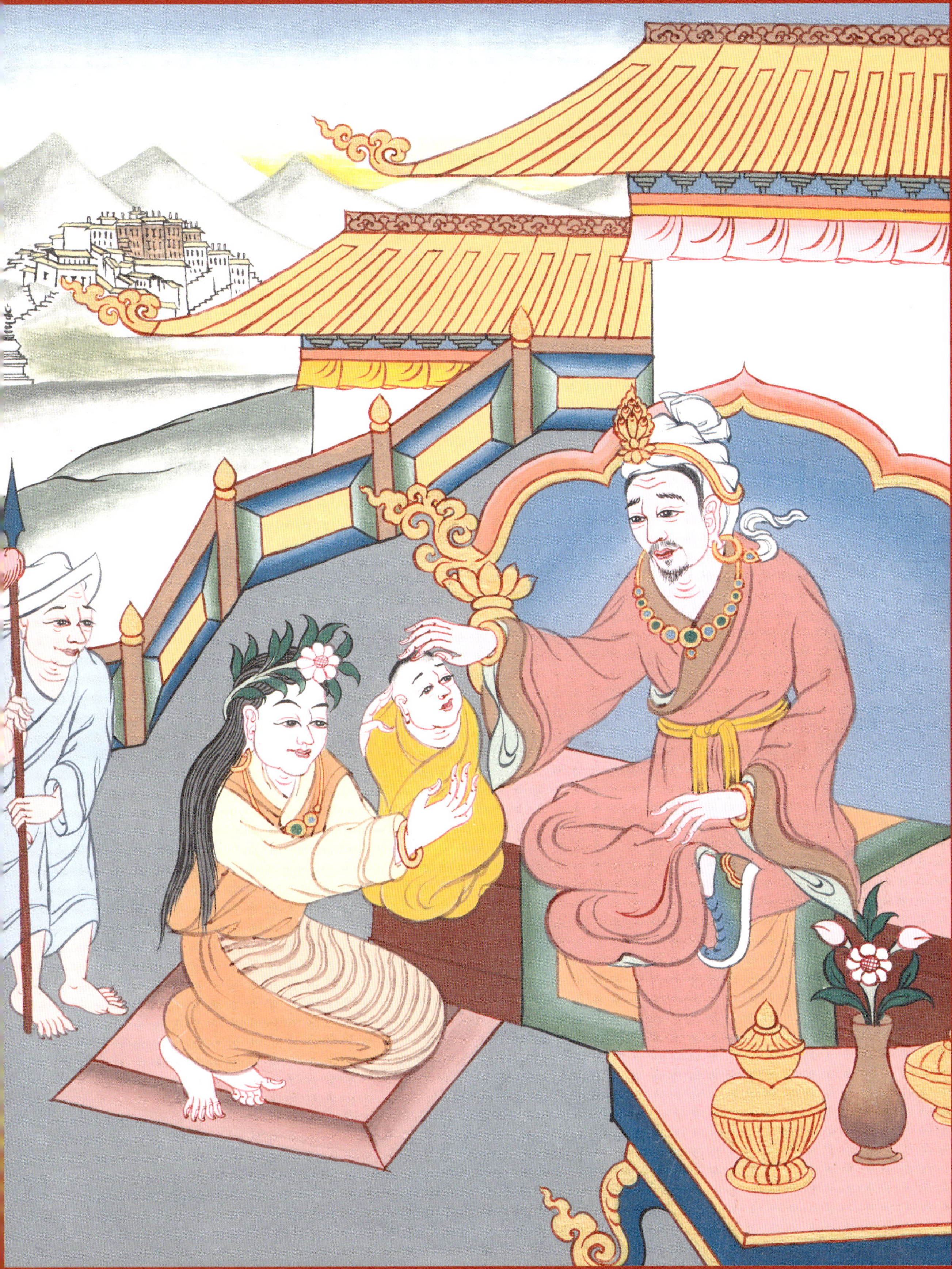

Seeing that both the people and the spirits were caught up in all kinds of imaginary conflicts, the heavenly buddha Manjushri was very sad. He decided that it would be much better if the Land of Snows with all its inhabitants, humans and spirits, could benefit from the Buddha's teaching. He also realized that the teachings had the potential to flourish here in this hidden country without being troubled by the rest of the world.

So from deep within the wisdom of his heart, Manjushri sent a ray of rainbow light down into the Land of Snows. It came to rest on the great castle of the king and queen and was absorbed. Soon after, the king and queen had a son with special qualities, named Trisong Detsen, who became the king of the Land of Snows when he was thirteen years old.

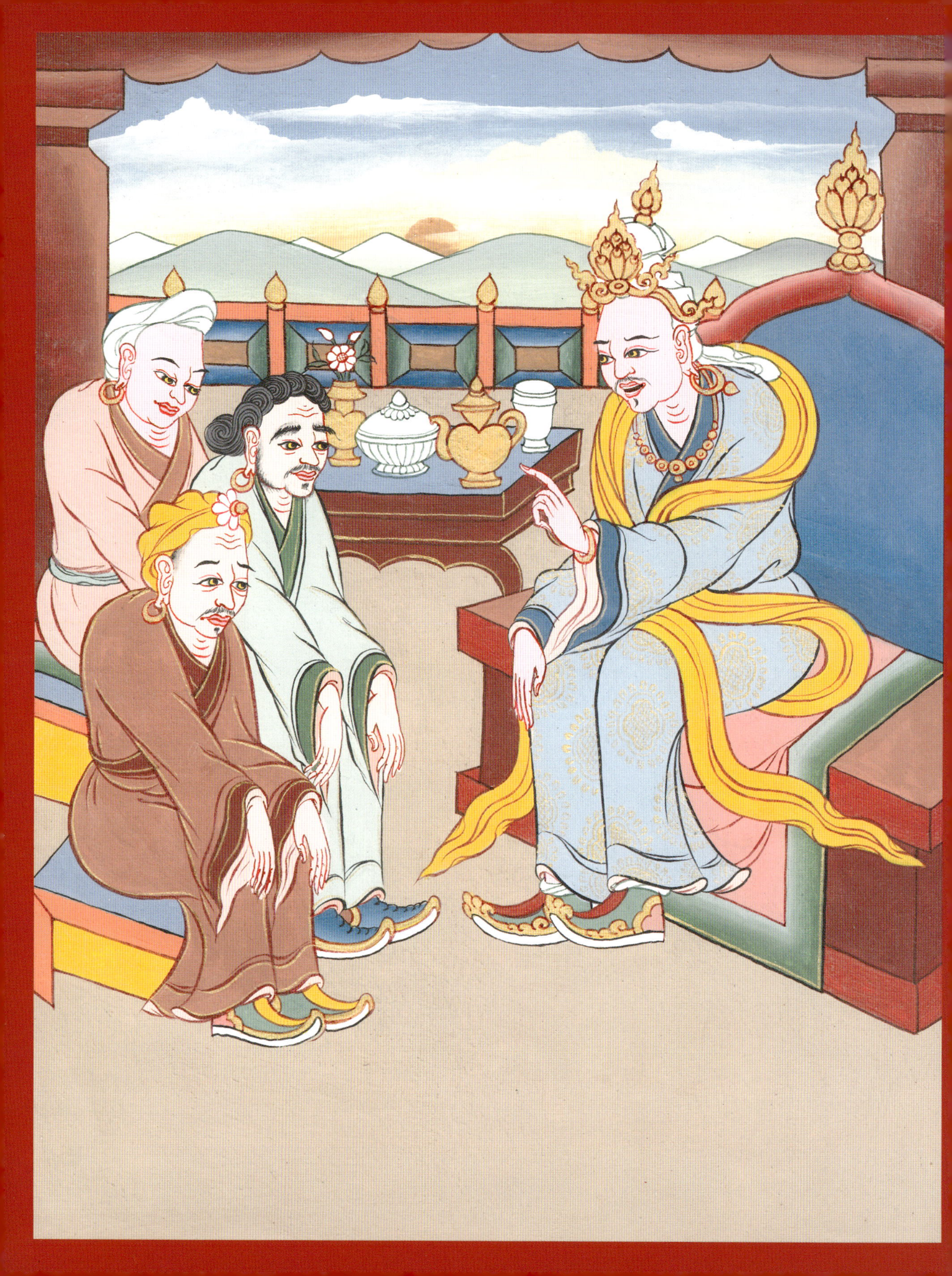

11

THE KING'S PLAN

As king, Trisong Detsen saw the same problems with the people and spirits of his kingdom that Manjushri had seen, and he was very sad about it for the same reasons. Not that the people were bad. In fact, basically they were very good, but sometimes—too often—they got confused. When that happened, they started thinking and doing things they didn't even really want to think or do. King Trisong Detsen desperately wanted happiness for them, so he decided to do everything in his power to establish the Buddhist teachings in the Land of Snows. He thought the Buddha's teachings would lead people away from violence and greed, bringing harmony to his kingdom. So he pondered long and hard about the best way to make that happen.

The big problem the king faced was that most of his people were not ready to accept the truth of the Buddha's teachings. Many were poor and had to work hard for a living. Most of the richer people had their minds on increasing their power, wealth, and advantages in their feuds. Rich or poor, most people didn't want to deal with anything strange or new. The spirits felt pretty much the same as the people did. They were very jealous of their territory. They liked their own particular style of doing things and didn't want any interference from the Buddha's teaching.

King Trisong Detsen developed a plan. Knowing that his kingdom had the shape of a female demon lying on her back, he planned to build a big, beautiful temple over the demoness's heart. He was sure that having the temple built right on the heart of the country, once it was properly blessed, would affect the whole kingdom in a deep way. He thought it would open the hearts of his people and compel the unruly spirits, gods, and demons of the Land of Snows to behave well and support the Buddha's teaching.

But getting the temple built was not going to be easy. To build it, the king needed considerable funds and the support of his ministers, who wielded great power. The ministers, like the spirits, were against anything new that might challenge their power. Many ministers were against Buddhism. They held the ancient local beliefs and feared that which was new. On top of that, Buddhist teachers came from other countries, India and China, and the ministers were very suspicious of them. They didn't trust foreigners and their ideas.

So King Trisong Detsen came up with a clever trick to get the ministers' support for the temple. He called them all together and reminded them that, in the past, each king of the Land of Snows had built important monuments for the people of the country to remember them by. He announced that he would also like to do this. To get the ministers on his side and make building the temple seem like their own choice, he gave them a list of possible projects and told them they could decide which one to carry out. They could choose to make a gigantic bronze pipe to hold the great and wide Brahmaputra River, which flows through the Land of Snows; build a castle so high that from the top of it you could see over the mountains into other countries; fill a huge canyon with gold dust; or build a small Buddhist temple near the capital of the country (where the heart of the demoness was). Of course, the ministers had to agree that the easiest and least expensive thing to do was to build the small Buddhist temple, and so the temple became their official choice.

Getting the ministers' approval was a big step forward for Trisong Detsen, but he knew that some of them could be fickle and tricky, and he worried that they might go back on their word. So he decided to secretly start building the temple without the ministers knowing about it. Once the temple was started, he thought, the ministers would no longer be able to change their minds.

But the king did not want to start this venture alone. He needed witnesses to spread the word once the construction had begun. He couldn't take any of the ministers with him or anybody else who might have bad thoughts about the Buddha's teaching. The king pondered this problem long and hard, as he always did when he had a problem, and at last he had a wonderful idea. He thought, *I'll take a group of children with me! The hearts of children are open. They are always ready for new things, and they are naturally joyful. They will be just the right company, and they can keep a secret—for a very short time anyway.*

So on King Trisong Detsen's twenty-first birthday, he took a group of children, including some of the ministers' and his own, to the special spot where the temple was to be built. When they reached the right place, the king put on his best white silk robe and told the children,

"This is a very important moment. We're going to do a great thing, but I need your help to succeed."

He got the children laughing and singing and dancing all around him. Then, with a great golden ax he began cutting into the ground the outline for the great temple. This took many hours, because unlike what he had told the ministers, the temple was to be quite large. Some of the children became tired and some even went to sleep, but the king kept working with the golden ax. When he was done, the exact shape of the temple was clearly marked in the ground and the king had all the children as witnesses of his activity.

When they got back to the capital, it was time for the children to tell the secret of where they had been and what they had been doing. First, they told their parents, then the parents told their friends, and soon everybody in the kingdom knew that the great temple had already been started. Now the king was sure that the ministers could never change their minds, no matter what obstacles and difficulties lay ahead.

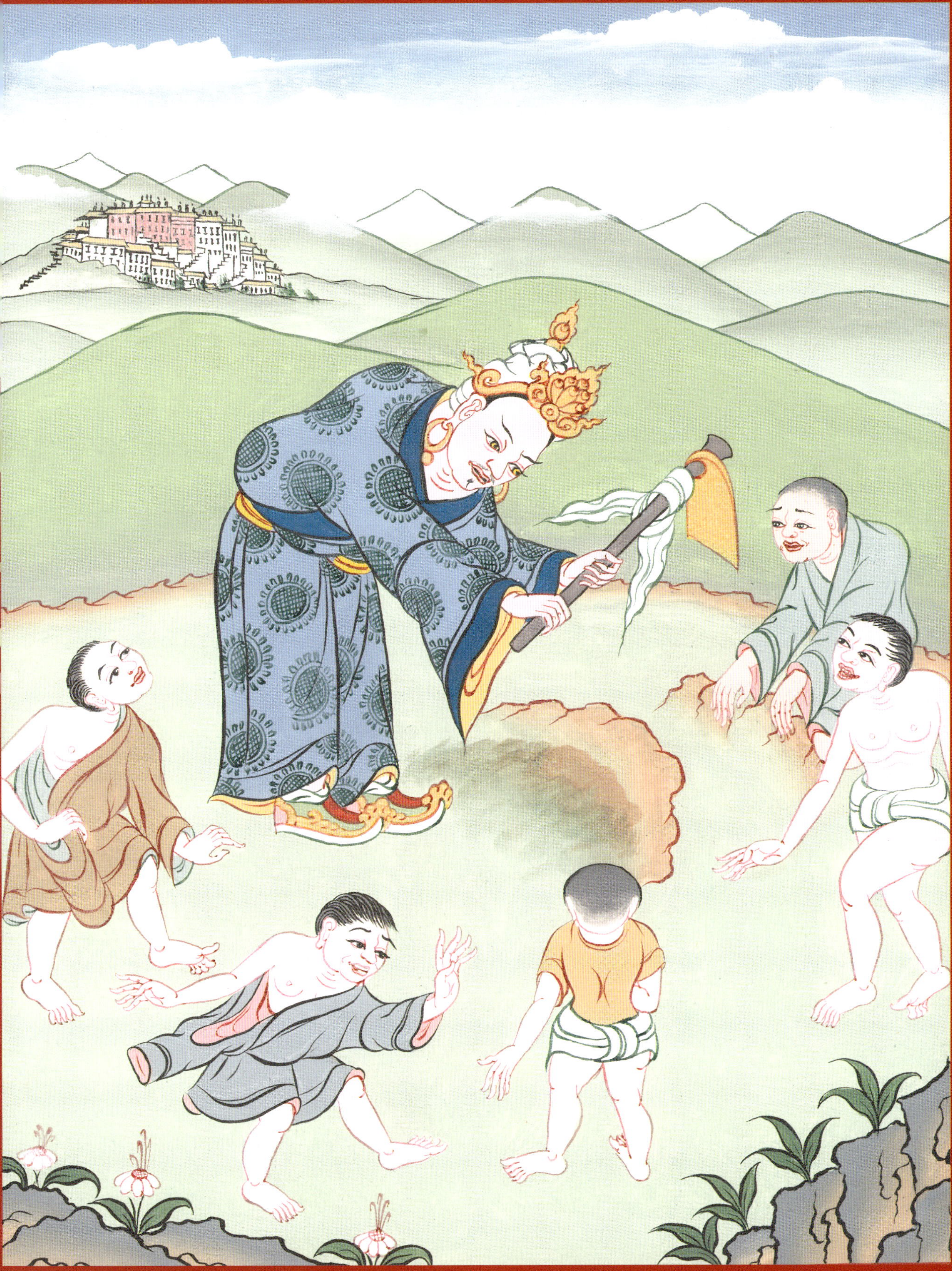

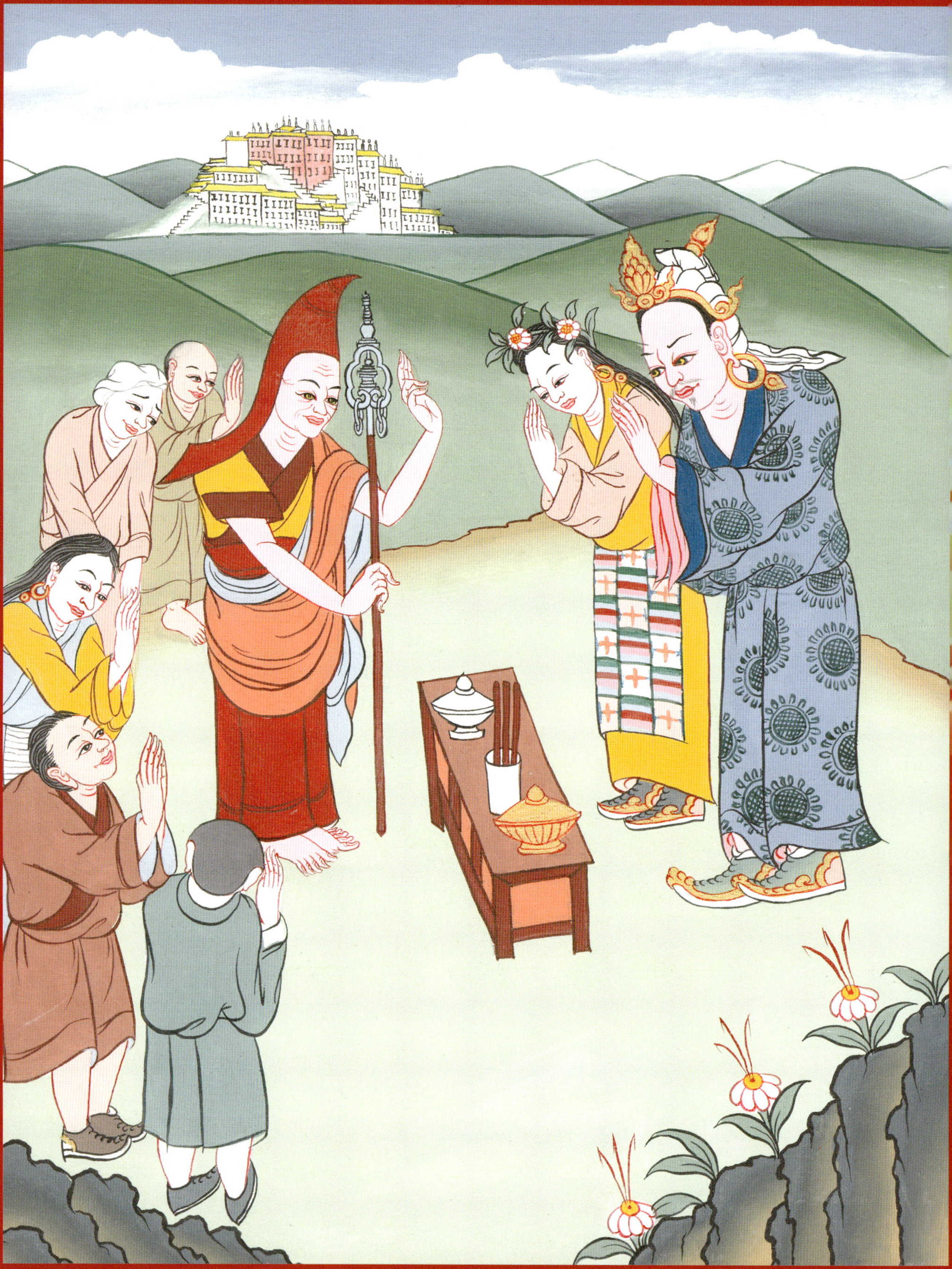

12

MASTER BODHISATTVA

The next step for the king was to find a Buddhist teacher to oversee the construction of and bless the temple. He had heard of a great teacher called Master Bodhisattva, who lived far to the south in the land of India. He was a master of the Buddha's teaching of kindness and love for all beings. This is called *compassion*, which means having your heart open to other people and putting them before yourself. A person who has real compassion has a great deal of power to open other people's hearts and make them kind and full of caring for others, too. This power to open people's hearts is called *the power of blessings*.

Strangely enough, blessings work on places as well as people. And the king wanted the temple to be full of blessings for all the people who came there. So the king sent for Master Bodhisattva to come from India, up through the high mountains to the country of the Land of Snows. Although this was a very hard journey to make and Master Bodhisattva was no longer a young fellow, he thought it was very important to help the Buddha's teaching take root in the Land of Snows. He reflected and thought, *This is my job; I am meant to do this.* So he decided to make the journey.

Master Bodhisattva came to the Land of Snows and gave his blessing to the place where the temple was to be built. King Trisong Detsen himself laid the first foundation stones, starting on the lines he had already cut into the ground with his golden ax. Then he had his builders come to continue the work.

As the building began, the spirits, gods, and demons of the Land of Snows became jealous and angry, as was their habit. They felt that this was their ground, and they did not want to lose it. Also, Master Bodhisattva's blessing had been so full of kindness and love that it had bruised their selfish hearts. So whatever the builders built during the day, the spirits tore down at night. Every morning when the builders came, they found the stones from the walls they had built the day before scattered on the ground.

Master Bodhisattva told the king, "All the power of my compassionate blessings has not been able to tame the savage gods and spirits of this place. It looks like they're not going to let us complete the temple."

The king was very upset. He shouted and stamped his foot. "We cannot give up now!" he said. "There must be something we can do." Impressed by the king's determination, Master Bodhisattva thought again as he paced around.

"Well, there is something, Your Majesty," he finally said. "We have to call on someone whose power in the Buddha's teaching is even greater than mine. It so happens that I know of a person like that. He is a completely Awakened One. He is the only one who can help us.

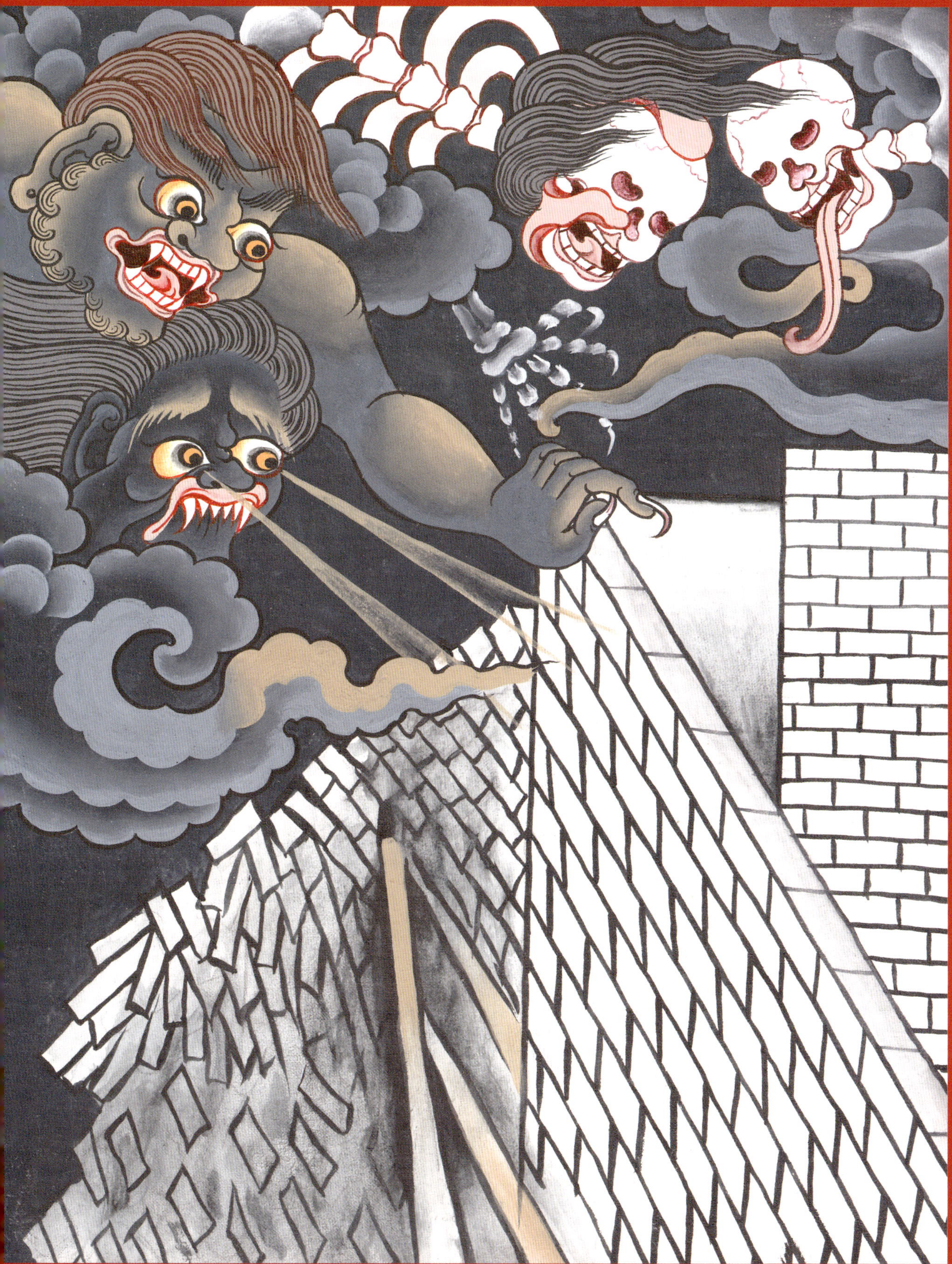

He is called Lotus-Born. He is a great meditator. He alone has the wrathful means to conquer the gods and demons of the Land of Snows."

"What do you mean by wrathful means?" asked the king.

"Kindness and caring for others are very powerful," replied Master Bodhisattva. "Such acts bring peace and harmony in most situations. But sometimes tougher action is required. When beings are very selfish, such as the nasty spirits here who keep destroying our work on the temple, kindness is not enough. Their eyes, ears, and hearts are closed; their meanness blots out everything. To wake such beings from their selfish dreams, they have to suffer a shock from a harsh power that is greater and bigger than their selfishness. Those gods and demons we are fighting have the power of the land and water, and even of the wind and rain—all that makes them very strong. But Lotus-Born has the power of the whole universe, and he is infinitely stronger than they are. He can give the gods and demons the shock they need to cut them down to size and make them serve the Buddha's teaching. That is the only way we are going to get this temple built."

"Lotus-Born is meditating in a secret cave far to the south, but I happen to know where that cave is," Master Bodhisattva said. "Let us send messengers to invite him. But listen here: This is something very important—you must tell your ministers that you had a vision of Lotus-Born in a dream. If they think you are following my instructions, they will be against the whole idea."

The next day, the king told everyone he had had a marvelous dream in which it had been revealed to him that in order to defeat the spirits and build the great temple, he must send for Lotus-Born, a powerful master of the Buddha's teaching who was meditating in Great Rock Cave far to the south. The story about the dream impressed the ministers. So messengers were sent to request Lotus-Born to come to the Land of Snows.

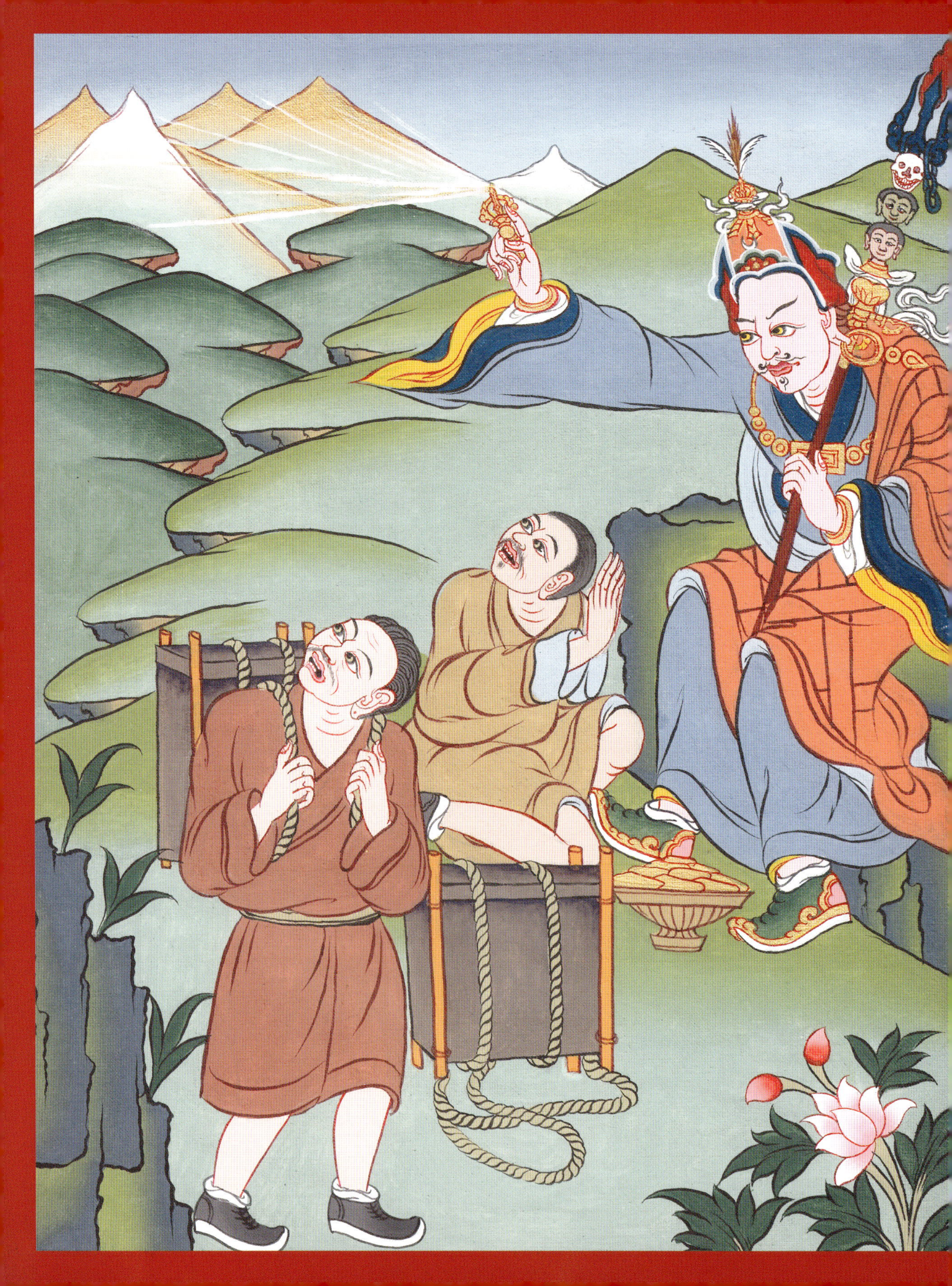

13

AN INVITATION

Lotus-Born was meditating in Great Rock Cave when he had a vision. A wisdom dakini appeared and told him, "Messengers are coming to you from the king of the Land of Snows. He needs your help to build a temple at the heart of his country. This is something you must do. But the messengers travel slowly, and they are already tired. It will take a long time for them to reach you, but they must make some effort, so go and meet them halfway."

So Lotus-Born flew through the sky to the halfway point. He got there much faster than the king's messengers. He had to wait there three months for them to arrive. When they finally got there, Lotus-Born asked them who they were, even though he already knew. They told him they were messengers from the king of the Land of Snows and made their request for help, offering him a large bag of gold dust.

"Give me more," said Lotus-Born.

They didn't have any more gold, so they stripped off their clothes and offered these to Lotus-Born.

"That's still not enough," he said.

"We have nothing else, so we offer you ourselves as your servants," they said and bowed down to Lotus-Born.

"Good, good. I was just testing you to see if I could really trust you," said Lotus-Born. "I don't need your gold. The whole world is gold for me."

With that, Lotus-Born stretched out his arm to one side and all the earth and rocks in that direction turned to jewels and gold. He stretched out his arm in the other direction, and the same thing happened on that side.

"Go ahead and take some," he said to the messengers. "Take as much as you can carry."

Using a special gaze, Lotus-Born then made the sun and moon sink to the ground. He made a particular kind of motion with his hand and a nearby river started flowing in the opposite direction. All this made a very big impression on the messengers. From then on, they treated Lotus-Born with great respect and awe and did whatever he said. So Lotus-Born agreed to go with them.

Lotus-Born's miracles also made the gods and demons of the Land of Snows perk up and take notice. Some of them sensed that a being of great power was coming to subdue them.

As Lotus-Born and the messengers moved deeper into the Land of Snows on their way to see the king, Mutsamey, the fearsome queen of the war gods of the west, attacked them. She took the form of two mountains and tried to crush Lotus-Born between them. But he only

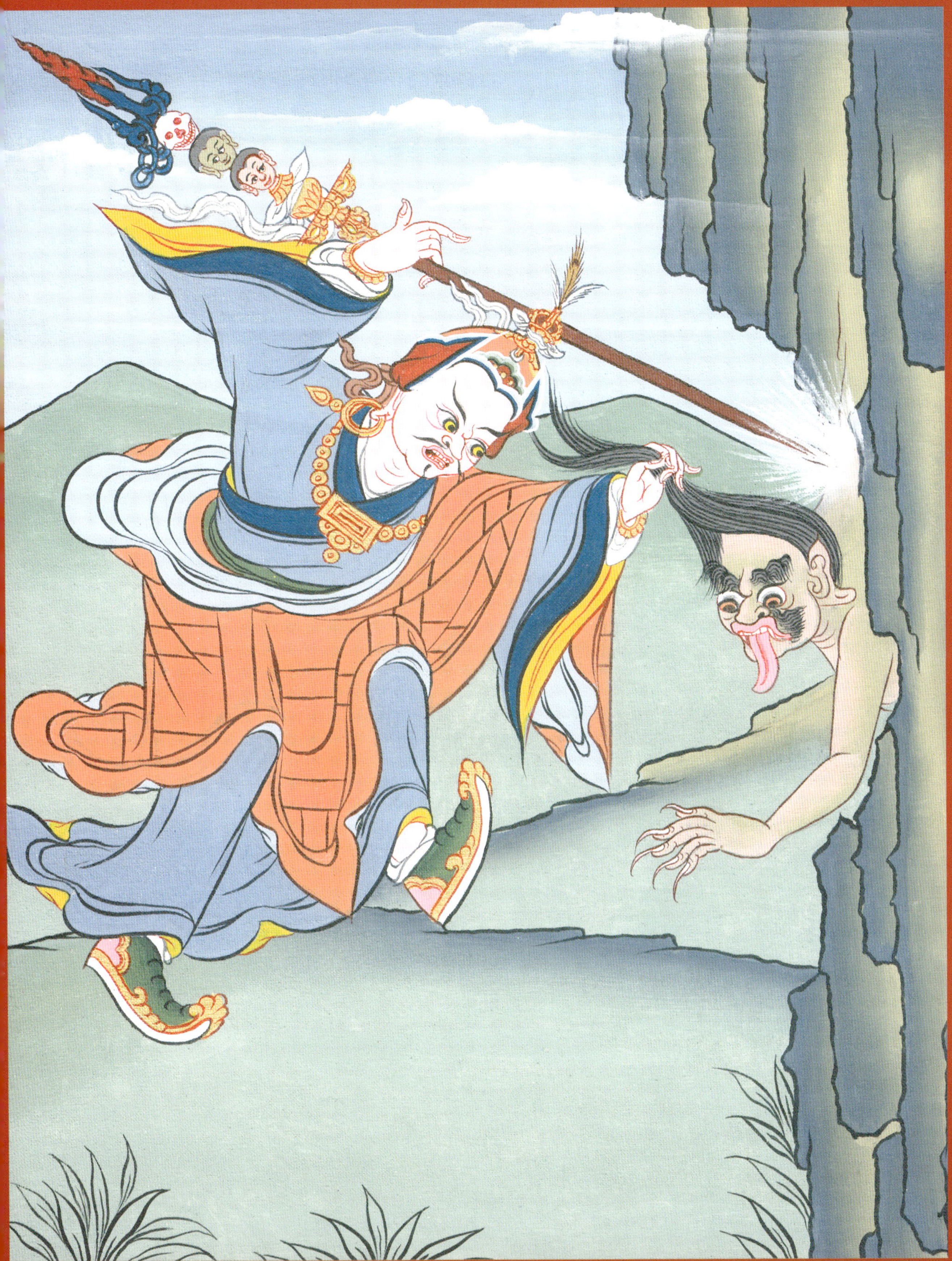

had to bang his stick on a rock to dissolve the two mountains and make the war goddess pop out in her bodily form and land on her head. She was very frightened of Lotus-Born's power. She swore to become his servant and from then on to protect the Buddha's teaching.

They hadn't gone much farther when the powerful goddess Nammen Karmo tried to strike Lotus-Born with lightning. He held up a small mirror and when the lightning struck it, it lost its power and fell to the ground as little burnt peas. Nammen Karmo was frightened, and she ran and jumped into a lake to get away from Lotus-Born. He formed his hand in the shape of a scorpion and made a gesture. The lake began to boil. It boiled all the flesh off the goddess's bones, and still, although nothing was left of her but her skeleton, she tried to run away. Lotus-Born threw his *vajra*, an indestructible metal thunderbolt that always came back to his hand, and it hit her in the eye. This was the end of Nammen Karmo's resistance. She gave up and swore to serve Lotus-Born and protect the Buddha's teaching from then on.

As Lotus-Born and the messengers continued on their way toward the capital of the Land of Snows to meet King Trisong Detsen, they were frequently attacked by spirits. Sometimes it was just one big powerful spirit, sometimes it was whole groups of them. There were male and female spirits. There were groups of demon sisters and groups of demon brothers. All the spirits and demons were trying desperately to destroy Lotus-Born before he took away their power. But this miraculous being had mastered the powers of the universe that lie beyond selfishness and self, and he easily defeated those who confronted him, making them swear to protect the Buddha's teachings forever. Still, there were more and more of them, and all of them were against Lotus-Born.

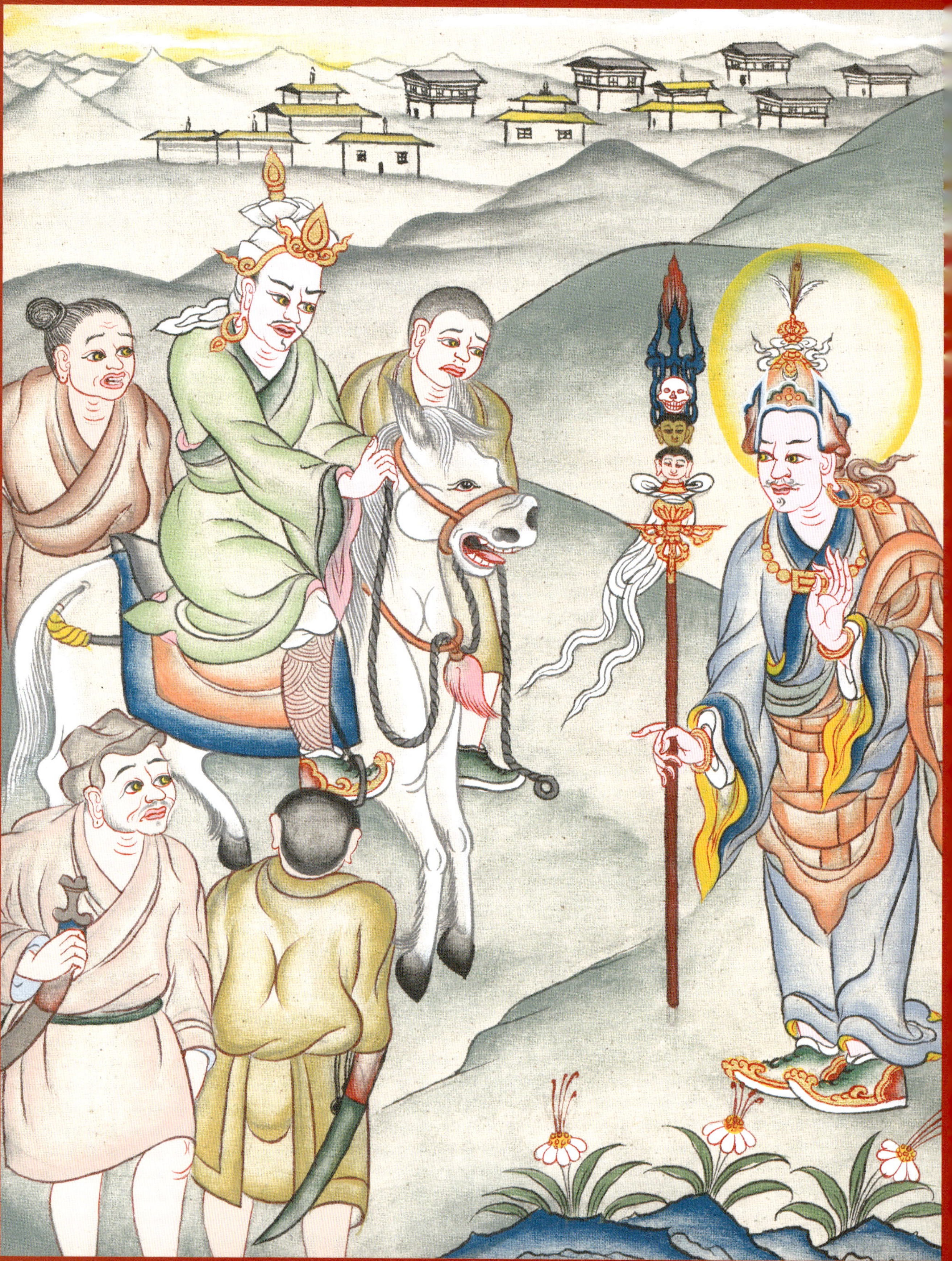

14

LOTUS-BORN ARRIVES

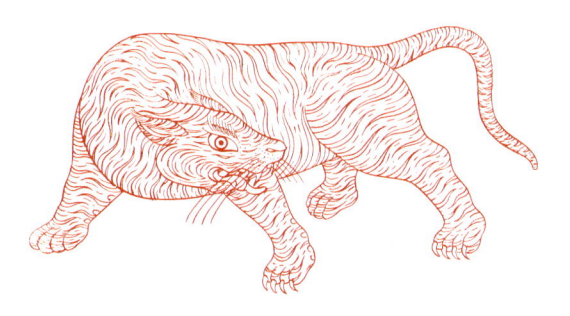

King Trisong Detsen and a group of his ministers rode out to meet Lotus-Born. The king, although he had very good intentions, was also rather proud. He thought, *I am the king.* And indeed, here he was, surrounded by ministers and servants, wearing fine clothes made of silk and riding a handsome steed. He thought, *When I meet Lotus-Born, he will bow down to me, and I will tell him what I want him to do.*

Soon Lotus-Born appeared with the king's messengers. They had journeyed a long way on foot and were travel-worn and ragged. Lotus-Born's ordinary clothes and dirty appearance gave no indication of his true power. The king remained sitting high up on his horse and waited for Lotus-Born to bow down to him.

Lotus-Born just stood there looking at the king, smiling slightly. He was quite handsome, with a thick black mustache, which he had grown while he was meditating in Great Rock Cave. His face was radiant, full of light.

"You should bow to me," the king finally said haughtily. "You are standing before a king."

But Lotus-Born was an Awakened One, which made him king of the universe, not just of one country on a small planet. He had traveled through many worlds, and the king had never even left the Land of Snows. Lotus-Born knew the king had to be taught a lesson.

"You may be the king of this little country hidden in the mountains, but you are ignorant and bloated with pride," said Lotus-Born. "You cannot even control your ministers, and you expect me, who has gone completely beyond the dreams of this world, to bow down to you? That is ridiculous. It is time for you to WAKE UP!" he shouted fiercely.

Lotus-Born raised one hand and a beam of light shot out at the king and scorched him all over, burning his clothes to black.

Quickly the king understood that he was face-to-face with somebody very great indeed and he better not fool around with this person. He fell to his knees on the ground and begged Lotus-Born for forgiveness.

"I forgive you," said Lotus-Born. "No ordinary person such as yourself can possibly understand who I am. You were right to bow down, but now you can get to your feet and tell me why you asked me to come here."

"I may be an ordinary person," said Trisong Detsen, "but I am the king of this nation. I care for my people, and I want them to benefit from the Buddha's teaching. That is why I called you here. I am trying to build a great temple that will help show everyone in this country that the Buddha's teaching is here, and here to stay. I want to build that temple right on the heart of the country so that its presence can be felt in every part of the Land of Snows. But the jealous gods and demons won't let me. They want to own the heart of the country. What we build during the day, they tear down at night. Master Bodhisattva told me you are the only one who can overcome them. I beg you to help."

"Ah, so," said the Lotus-Born. "That is a worthy cause, and taming demons is rather a specialty of mine. I will see what I can do. These stubborn gods and demons of yours shouldn't be much of a problem." The king was overjoyed, and he bowed down again many times. He invited Lotus-Born to come to his palace, where he held a great feast and offered Lotus-Born heaps of gold and jewels as gifts.

After the feast, Lotus-Born got right to work. He scanned the whole region in his mind and quickly saw where all the gods and demons were that had to be defeated. He saw that they were of three main kinds: those who lived high up, those who lived on the middle level, and those who lived in the low parts of the earth or down below the earth altogether. Some of the upper type were owners of mountains and lived on top of them. The middle ones lived on the slopes of mountains, mainly where there were lots of big rocks, especially red-colored rocks, and many of these middle-level spirits were red themselves and rode red horses. Others lived in lowlands, in lakes or rivers, underneath the earth, or even deep down under the lakes and rivers. Lotus-Born knew right away where they all were.

Those who wanted to fight, he easily defeated. Others he gave gifts, mostly things to eat or drink or things that smelled good. Some, especially the nagas who lived in the water, wanted gold and jewels. Those who didn't want to fight all had their price.

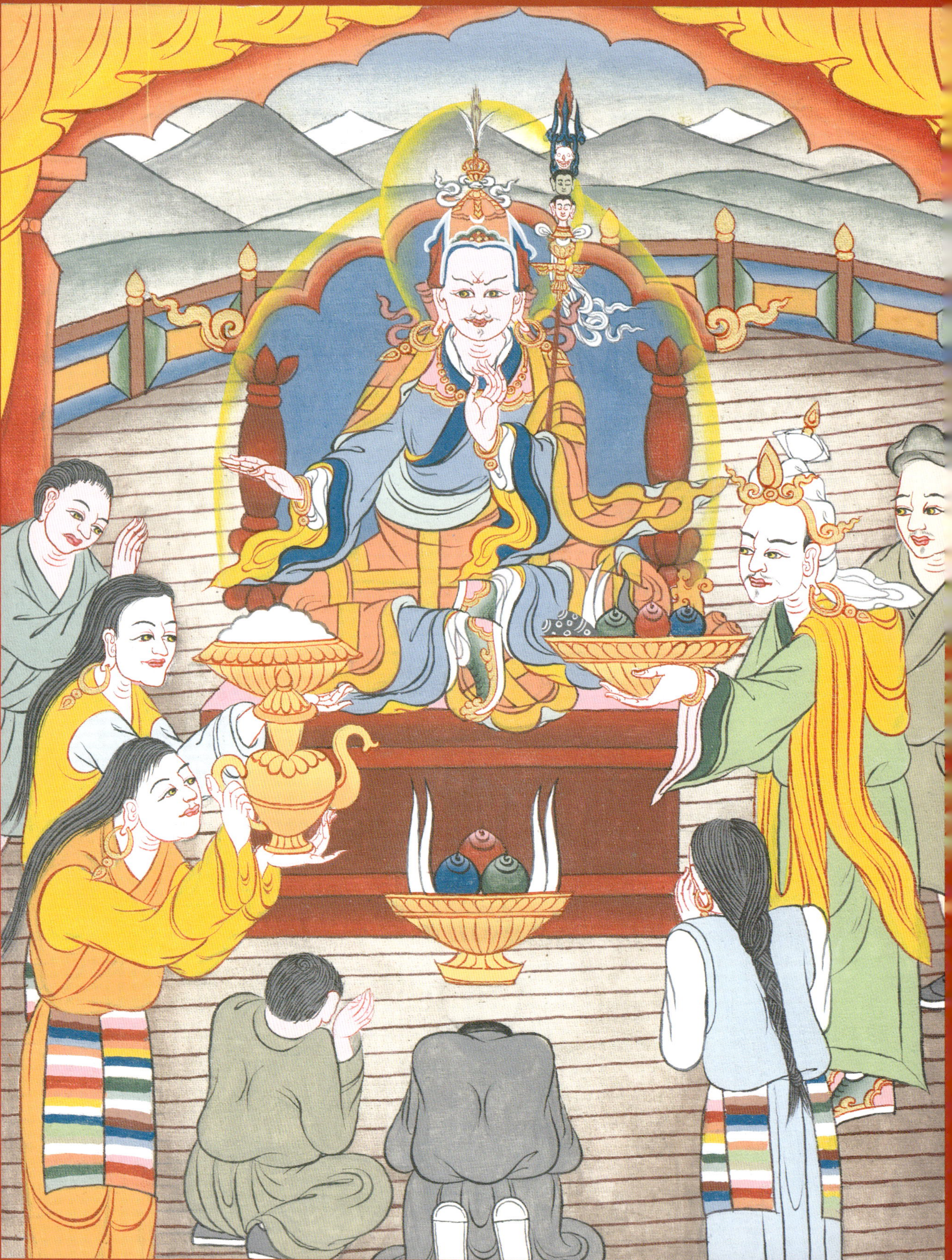

Soon all the spirits—all the gods and demons of various shapes and sizes, nasty and not so nasty—swore to Lotus-Born not to prevent King Trisong Detsen from building the great temple. Some of them even pledged to help him. Lotus-Born made all of them swear to serve the Buddhadharma.

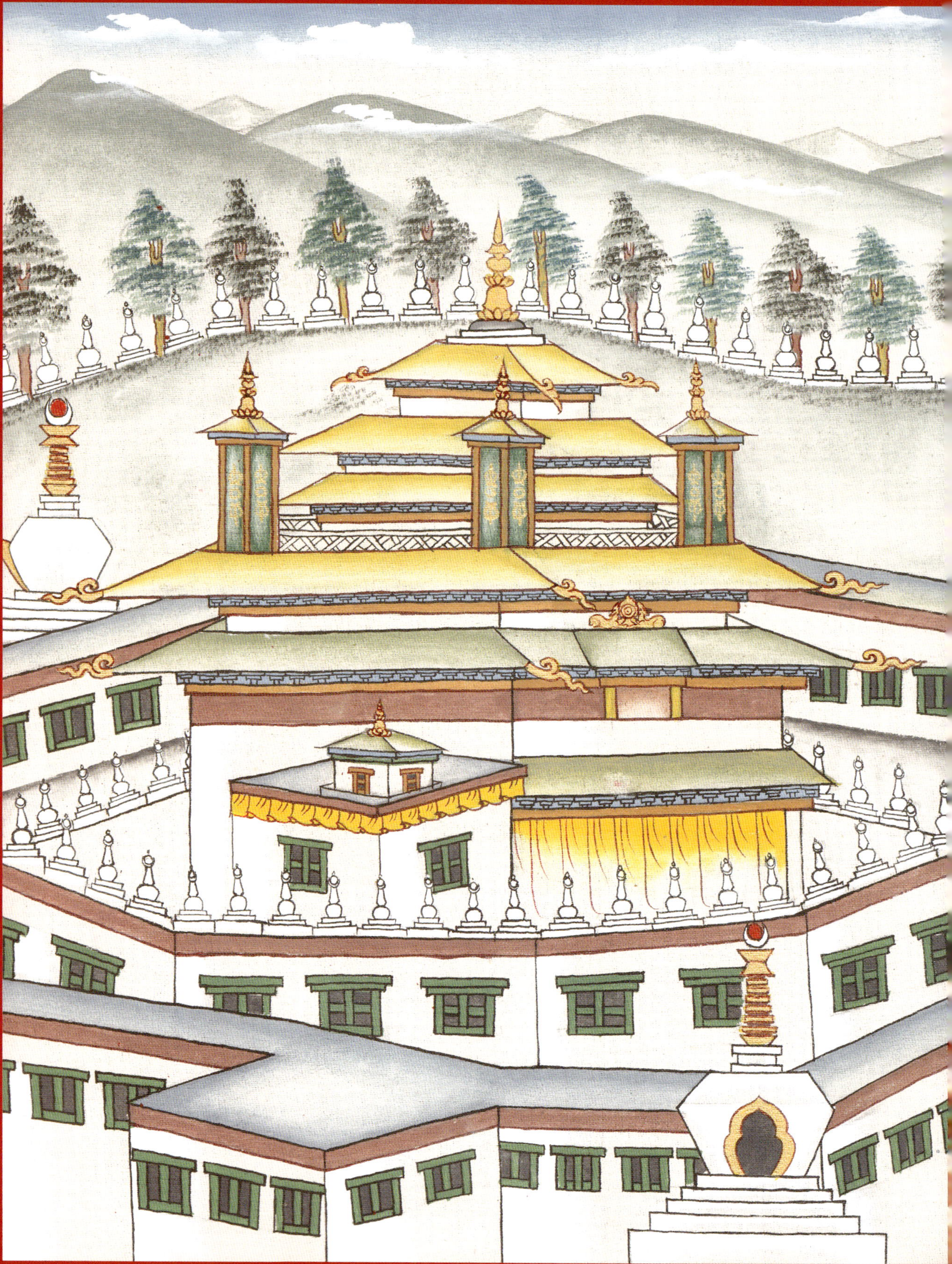

15

SAMYE IS BUILT

After Lotus-Born had subdued all of the malevolent spirits, the builders got back to work on the temple. It was to be called Samye, and it would be composed of many small temples and shrines. The humans employed by the king worked during the day. Then, during the night, the gods and demons did the building. The nagas floated the wood down the rivers at night, and in the morning, the carpenters found the amount they needed for their day's work waiting for them on the riverbank.

With Lotus-Born keeping close watch on them, humans and spirits all worked together, and the great temple was completed in five years. When it was all finally finished—sturdy, gleaming, and beautiful—a great feast was held with the king, his court, and hundreds of people from all over the Land of Snows. Lotus-Born and Master Bodhisattva blessed the temple and then taught from the rooftop to crowds of people listening below.

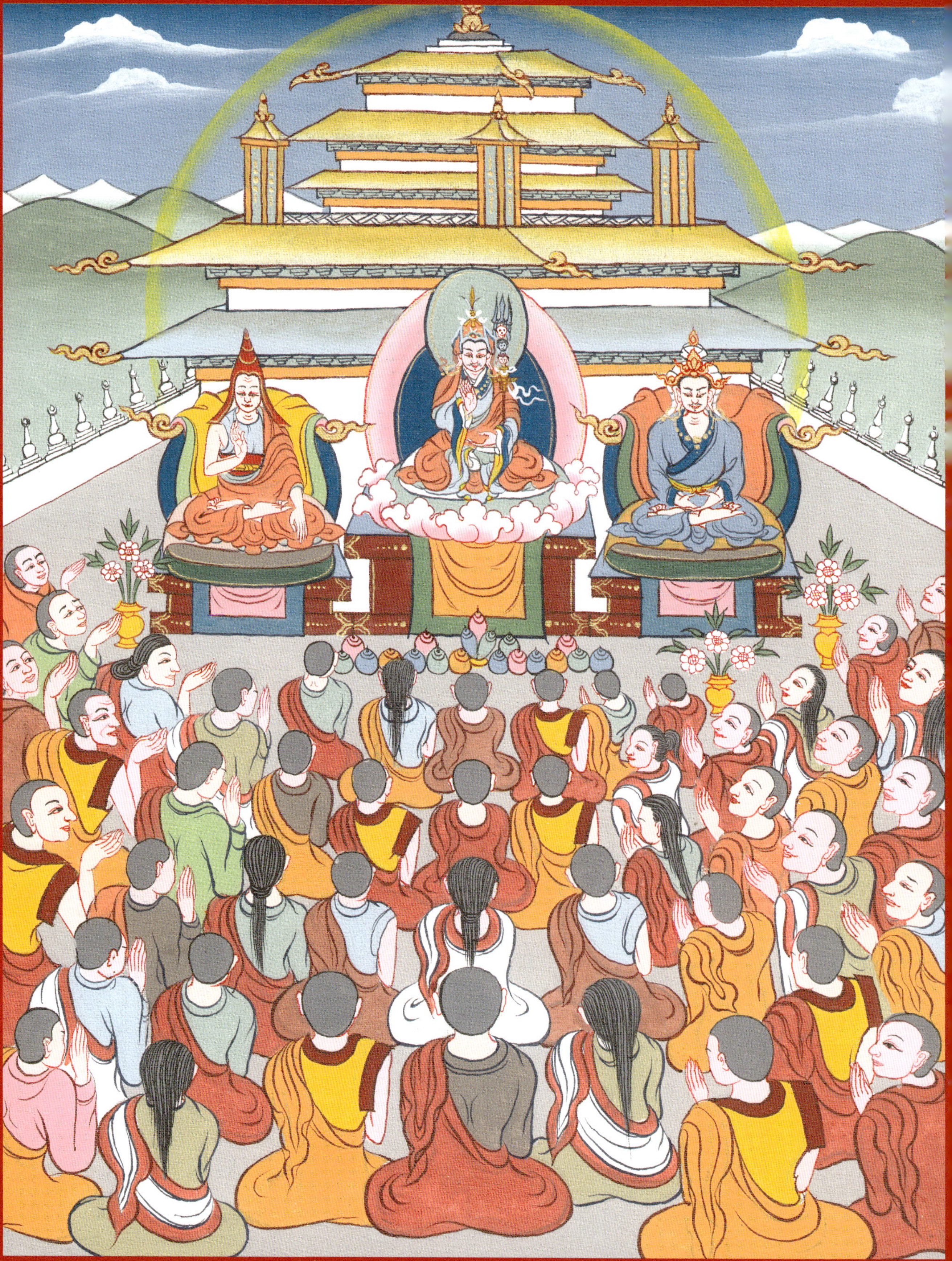

This great event changed the Land of Snows in favor of the Buddhist teachings. Everyone was in it together—the people and all of the gods and demons of the land, led by the king and guided by Lotus-Born and Master Bodhisattva. Everyone, that is, except the jealous ministers, who only became more nervous. They saw every success by Lotus-Born as a trick to increase his power and make the people love him more. They were afraid that once the people loved Lotus-Born enough, he could do whatever he wanted with the Land of Snows. They suspected he might put the country in the hands of foreigners or even proclaim himself king. These ministers feared that they would lose their lands and wealth and that they would no longer have any power in the kingdom. While pretending to be pleased by Lotus-Born's successes, they plotted in secret to destroy him.

Given that the temple was finished, the ministers told King Trisong Detsen that it was time to send the two masters, Lotus-Born and Master Bodhisattva, back to their home in India. But the king had great faith in the masters and instead begged them to stay on and teach. He and the people of the Land of Snows knew only a little bit about how to wake up. There was so much more to learn. The two great masters listened to the king's pleas and felt compassion for him and his people. They agreed to stay and teach.

But despite the enemy ministers' secrecy, Lotus-Born knew very well that they were constantly plotting against him. Now that he had agreed to stay, he figured they would redouble their efforts to destroy him. So he kept his eye on them. For their part, the ministers knew that Lotus-Born was watching them, and they plotted very carefully.

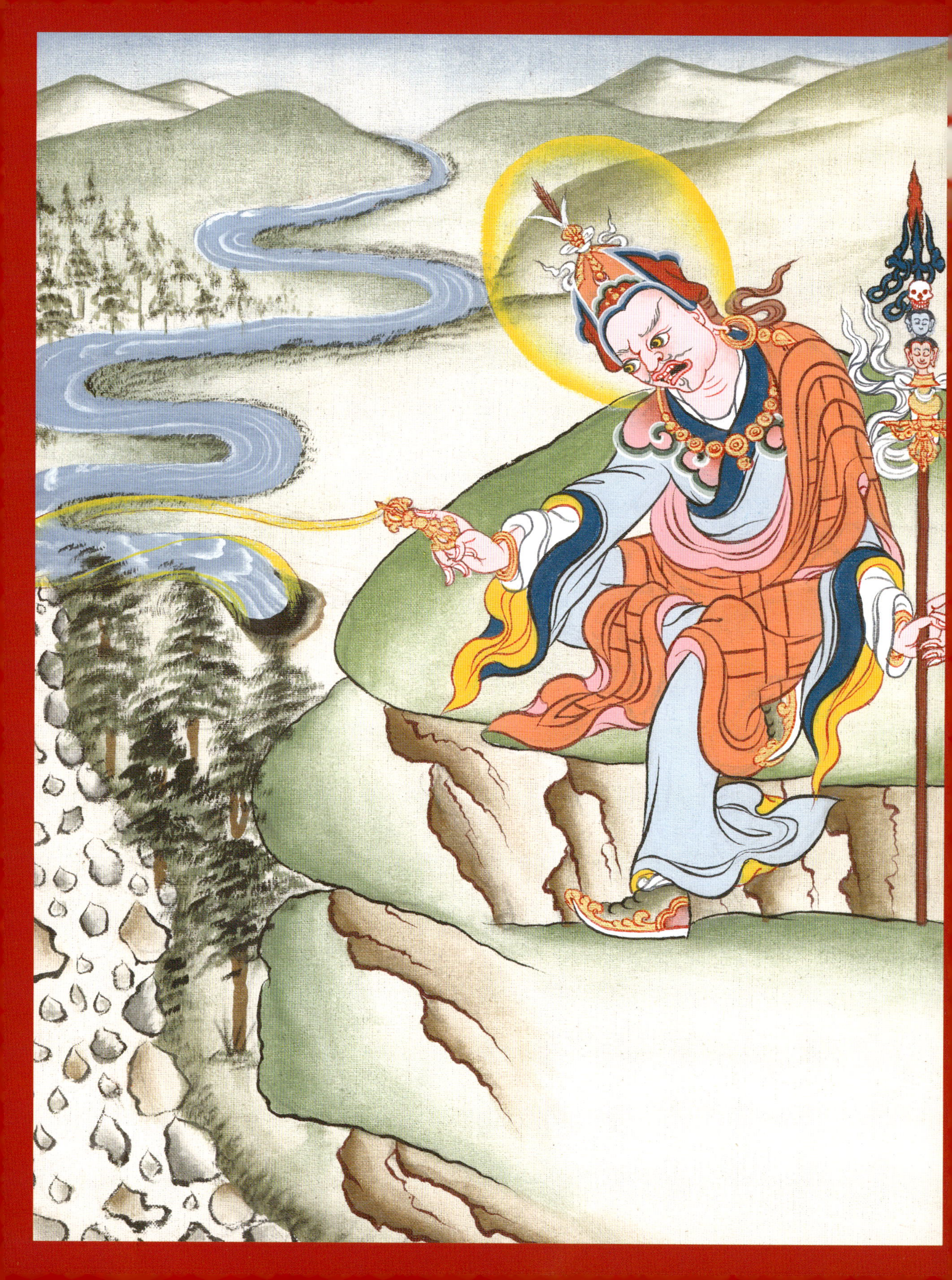

16

THE MINISTERS' DECEIT

During his stay, Lotus-Born found many ways to help the people of the Land of Snows. Though there was snow on the high mountains, much of the country was very dry. There was little water for humans and animals to drink, and there certainly wasn't enough water in many places for planting fields and growing crops. In those places, the land and hills were bare and rocky. There were only a few trees. Because of this, many of the people were poor and often hungry. But one of Lotus-Born's special powers was with water. He knew how to control it. He had power over the nagas, the water gods, and the elements themselves, so he could quickly sense where there was water running underground and bring it to the surface. He could change the direction of rivers and streams. He could make lakes overflow to irrigate the land around them. He could even make rain. So he went around the country turning vast areas of desert into beautiful fields for growing food and making lush forests grow overnight. More and more parts of the country became fertile and full of plant life, and the people who lived there became prosperous. Animals had plenty to eat, and herds became large and well fed.

This was wonderful for the Land of Snows, but it simply infuriated the ministers. They only saw it as another one of Lotus-Born's tricks to steal their power. They came up with a desperate scheme. They hired eighteen skilled and dangerous warriors to sneak up on Lotus-Born and attack him. Traveling only at night and keeping well hidden, the eighteen warriors followed Lotus-Born as he moved from camp to camp performing his water miracles. They knew Lotus-Born wouldn't be easy to kill, and they were waiting for just the right opportunity. One morning when Lotus-Born was working deep down in a ravine, they decided their moment had come. They crawled silently through the trees until they reached the edge of the ravine. When they had Lotus-Born clearly in view just below them, they came out from behind the trees shouting their war cries, throwing their spears, and shooting their arrows.

Of course, Lotus-Born had known they were there the whole time. He had not paid much attention to them because they were really no threat to him. When they attacked, he simply raised his hand in a gesture of power and froze all the warriors on the spot. They instantly stood motionless in their places, their swords and spears raised, their bows drawn, and their mouths wide open in mid-shout. But they were perfectly silent. They were slowly turning to stone.

Now that Lotus-Born had rendered the warriors motionless in the midst of their ambush, everybody could plainly see the ministers' treachery. The frozen warriors were the unmistakable proof of their guilt, which they could no longer hide. And because their evil plotting could now be clearly seen by everyone, King Trisong Detsen was able to denounce them and send them away.

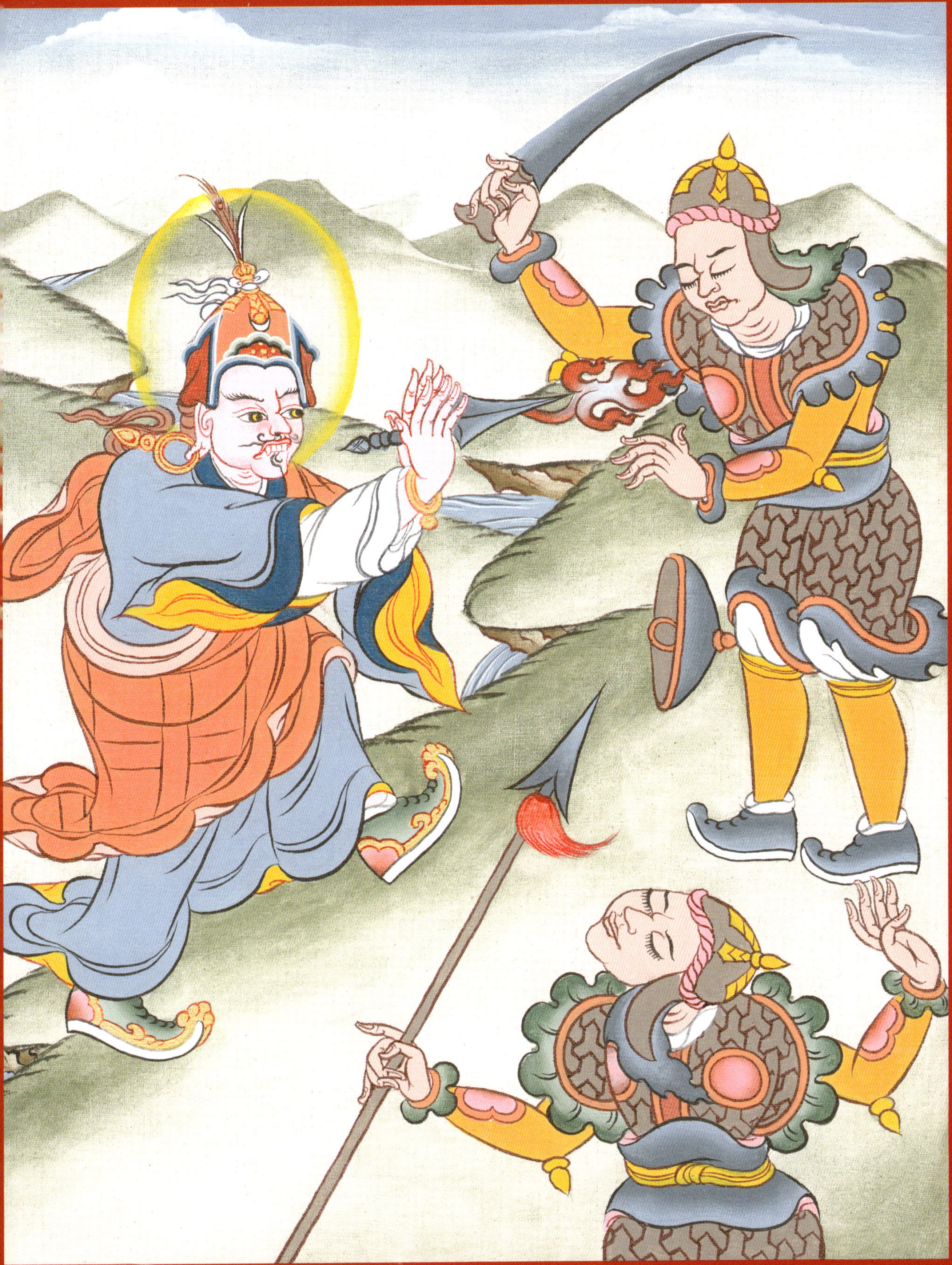

The king had wanted to do this for a long time. These evil ministers had always stood in the way of his attempts to establish the Buddhist teachings in the Land of Snows, but the ministers had had too many supporters for the king to fire them. Now their supporters had no choice but to admit that the ministers were guilty of treason. The king banished them from the capital. The ministers had been right that they were going to lose their positions and power because of Lotus-Born, but they had done it to themselves through their own evil schemes.

Once the frozen warriors were no longer needed as proof, Lotus-Born decided to save them. He cast a spell on a bag of mustard seeds and sent a messenger to sprinkle the seeds on the motionless warriors. As soon as the blessed seeds fell on them, they came back to life and walked away wondering what in the world had happened to them. They were grateful to Lotus-Born for sparing their lives. If he had not had compassion on them and sent the messenger with the mustard seeds, those warriors would still be standing on the edge of that ravine today.

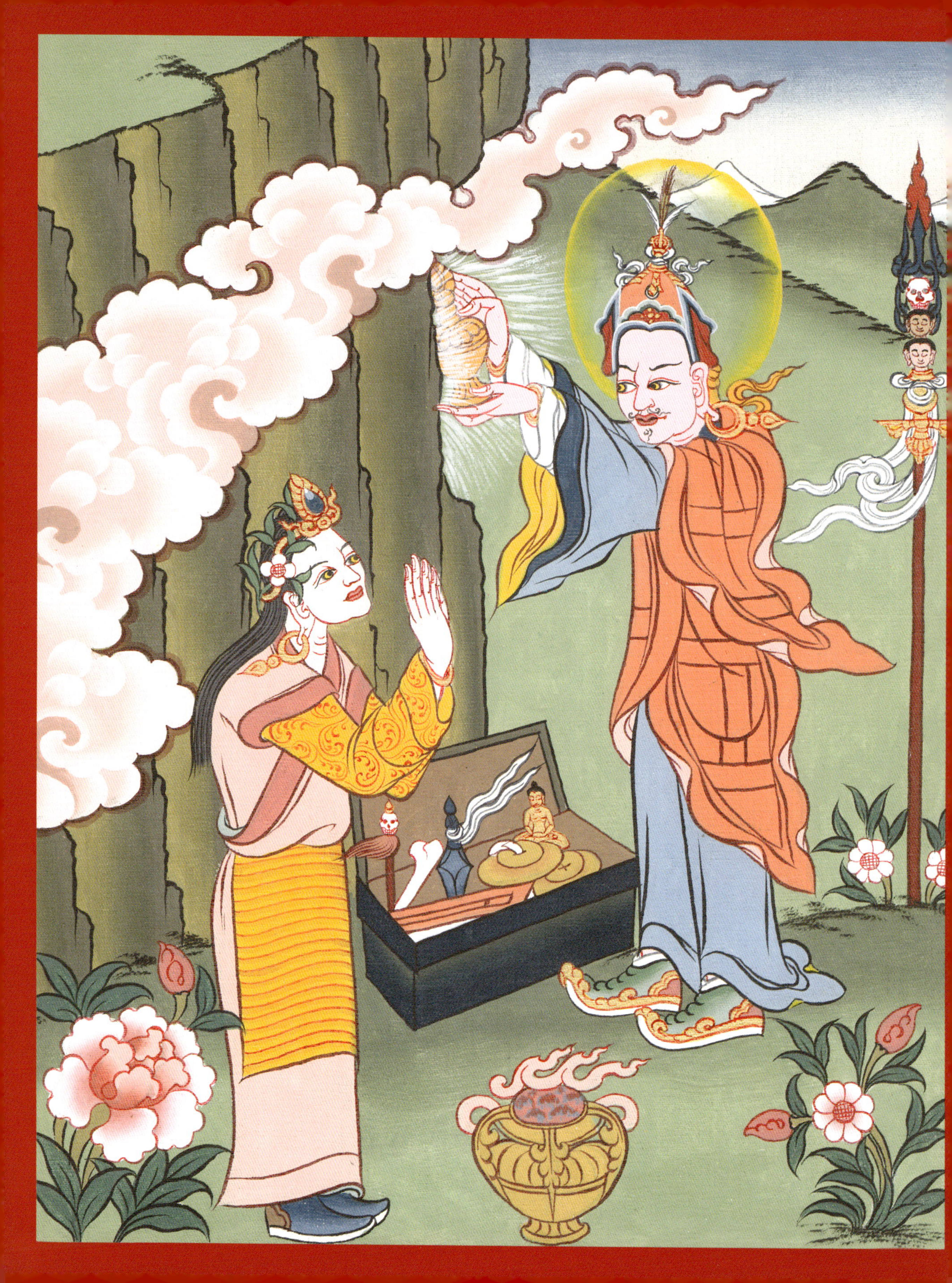

17

LOTUS-BORN'S LEGACY

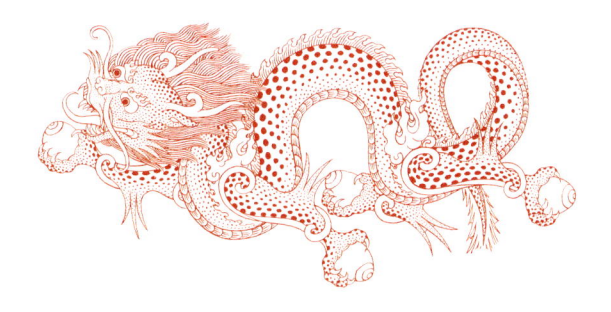

With the ministers no longer in the way, King Trisong Detsen, Lotus-Born, and Master Bodhisattva were able to establish Buddhism in the Land of Snows unhindered. Through his instruction, many of Lotus-Born's students became Awakened Ones themselves. There were twenty-five in particular who were considered the most accomplished. One of them, Namkai Nyingpo, could fly through the air. Yeshe Tsogyal, who was perhaps the closest, had perfect memory and could even bring the dead back to life.

    Lotus-Born knew that his students would have students, and those students would have students after them, allowing the special teachings on awakened mind and compassion to be passed down through generations in the Land of Snows. He was very happy about this, but he also knew that eventually things would change. Dark times would come, in which the teachings could be lost, so he wrote them down in many different forms. He hid these writings for the people of future dark ages, so they could be discovered when the time was right. Sometimes he wrote on paper with invisible ink. Sometimes he wrote in dakini language, which only very special people could read. Sometimes he magically carved his writings into jewels buried in small boxes. He hid these writings in many places all over the Land of Snows—inside rocks, under temples, in caves, on mountaintops, in riverbeds. He even hid them in other worlds. And for hundreds of years, at the right moments, people have discovered them, even up to the present time.

As everyone around him, including Master Bodhisattva and King Trisong Detsen, became old and died, Lotus-Born didn't age, because he had learned the secret of living forever without aging. After many years of activity in the Land of Snows, when the country was ruled by King Trisong Detsen's son Mutig Tsenpo, Lotus-Born decided that it was time to move on.

"It is time for me to leave the Land of Snows," he said. "I have established the teachings here and helped the humans and animals of this country in many ways. Now I am needed in another world called Chamara. There are cannibal demons living there that will eventually attack the world of humans if they are not subjugated and tamed. I must now go to that world in order to save the humans of the future."

Mutig Tsenpo and all his ministers and courtiers were heartbroken and begged Lotus-Born not to abandon them.

"You are our great teacher and protector," said the king. "Please do not leave us. How can we ever get along without you!"

But Lotus-Born was firm.

"I must go, Your Majesty," he said. "I have important work to do. Please do not try to stop me."

"Then at least let us ride along with you for a while," begged the king, "so we have time to get used to the idea of saying goodbye to you. It would be too hard to do so immediately."

Because he loved the people of the Land of Snows very much, Lotus-Born agreed to this. It so happened that he had to ride several days to the south in order to reach the point from which he could travel to the other world. He told the king and his retinue that they could accompany him that far.

And so Lotus-Born with the king and a large procession rode together for the next several days with flags flying, drums beating, and crowds of loyal demons and spirits accompanying them unseen in the air and under the ground. From time to time the procession would stop and Lotus-Born would answer the people's questions. He gave them advice about the practical things in their lives and even more advice on how to run the kingdom so that all the people could live well. At this time, he offered his primary student and confidant, Yeshe Tsogyal, his special iron dagger as a symbol of entrusting her as the keeper of his teachings.

At last they reached the place from which Lotus-Born was to leave. Miraculously, a great beam of rainbow-colored light shot down from the sky, and Lotus-Born mounted it. The people were astonished and many of them began to cry, knowing that Lotus-Born was about to finally leave them.

"Farewell, Your Majesty. Farewell, dear people," said Lotus-Born, sitting on the light beam and holding aloft his vajra thunderbolt scepter. "I am leaving you now to go defeat the cannibal demons. It should not take me very long, maybe just a few of your years. After that, I will make my home there on the island of Chamara, where I can keep the cannibal demons under control. My palace will be on top of the great copper-colored mountain in the middle of that island. Call to me there when you are in need. I will always hear you—not only the king but any of you. You will always have my help."

Sitting miraculously astride the rainbow, Lotus-Born looked more elegant and beautiful than ever. As the light beam carried him off to another world, he looked back at the people with an unforgettable radiant smile.

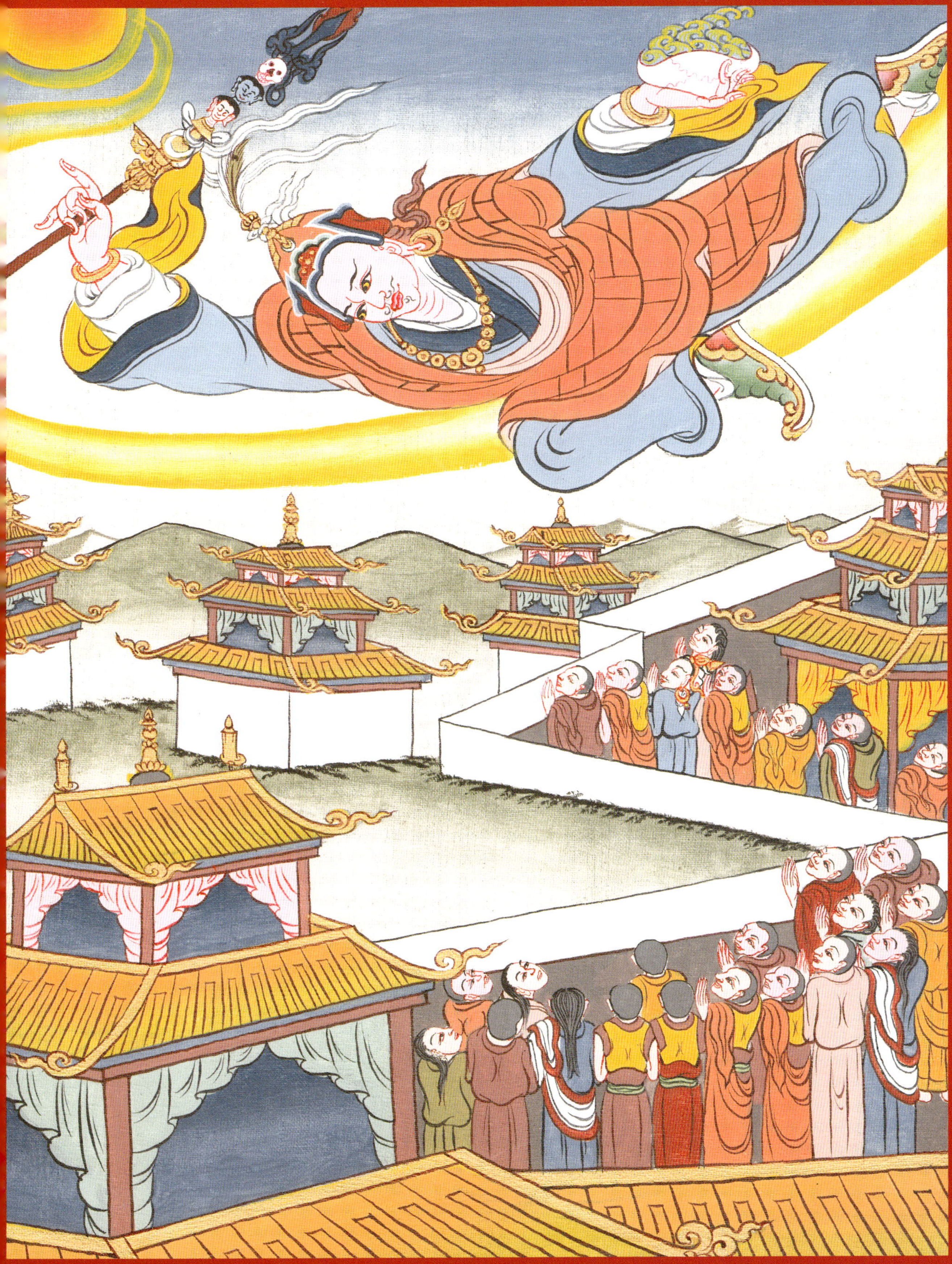

AFTERWORD
Dzongsar Khyentse Rinpoche

I am so happy that this amazing story of the Lotus-Born, Guru Padmasambhava, is now available in English for children. Even though the historical Lotus-Born might have never been to the West, his way of being and living is actually more relevant than ever to our modern world, and completely accessible to a Western audience of all ages.

One can get a good education in Western schools and universities, and perhaps even learn everything that is teachable. But is that all there is? Don't conventional education and even reason have their limits? How can one complete one's training? Is there something to learn that cannot be taught? How do we loosen our tight grip on what we think is believable, or for that matter, what we think is unbelievable? Do we dare step into the unconventional, the unknown, the unbelievable, and a zone of discomfort?

I know no better way to take that daring step than to let Guru Padmasambhava inspire us and to let him show us precisely the wisdom and truth that cannot be taught. Guru Padmasambhava appeared in our world and in our minds to show us that being able to touch, feel, and see the walls of our tiny mental boxes is the very proof that there must be so much more to discover on the other sides of those walls.

To begin with, Guru Padmasambhava was born from a lotus. He could easily have been born from a marigold instead. But according to ancient Indian mythology, the lotus is special because, though it abides in thick mud, it is so beautiful, fascinating, and totally dirt-resistant—never stained by the mud. That is the stainless wisdom of the Lotus-Born that can't be taught by our schoolteachers but for which we long with all our hearts.

The good news is that this is not just a storybook about someone who lived long ago and far away. By letting this story enter our hearts and lives, we really can discover Guru Padmasambhava's wisdom in ourselves. Though his feats may seem magical and amazing, actually he and his wisdom have never been separate from us.

So why don't we "see" with wisdom? What is the mud that obscures our vision? We will be able to answer these questions when we remember that Guru Padmasambhava was born in the monkey year. With all due respect to our hairy friends in the jungle, monkeys tend to not sit still on one single spot. They like to run around, jump, and swing from tree to tree, up and down, left and right, back and forth—always very, very active, speedy, and constantly restless. If you were to leave them alone in your kitchen for just one hour, they would create an utter mess.

Our normal thinking minds are just like that—never still, always jumpy, ready to be distracted at any time. Sometimes we even call it our *monkey mind*. And yet, in the midst of this muddy mind—the distracted, wild, limited, and obscured monkey mind—the Lotus-Born miraculously appears. Suddenly he shows us an amazing opportunity to be different in the way we think, talk, and act—different in our whole way of being.

That is what this book and the life of Guru Padmasambhava are all about. Guru Padmasambhava is, of course, not the goal, but he is like the finger pointing at it: he shows us so many different ways to find that inner truth and wisdom we all have. Usually we say that he manifests in eight different ways: for example, sometimes he is peaceful, sometimes wrathful, sometimes elegant or serene, and sometimes outrageous—whatever he needs to do to solve different types of problems or to reach different types of people with different habits and hang-ups.

One of our favorite human habits is, unfortunately, our love of getting into trouble. Even though intellectually we claim to prefer happiness and troublelessness, our own experiences have taught us otherwise: our habits have the opposite effect. The story of Guru Padmasambhava shows us that whenever our minds get muddied by our old habits, the Lotus-Born will always be happening right there to wake us up. So again, this book really is not a story about someone who did miraculous things far away and long ago. Actually, Guru Padmasambhava is right here, right now, all the time.

Whenever those gluey pieces of mud start to stick together and make us depressed and lonely, afraid or insecure, angry, greedy, or jealous, just thinking of Guru Padmasambhava can wake us up and bring us back to true wisdom. This truth of Guru Padmasambhava is always available to us, beyond all the usual limitations of culture, convention, gender, sexual orientation, politics, race, space, or time. And this book is a beautiful way to introduce children to the wisdom that is their natural birthright.

Since forgetting this fact is a by-product of our trouble-loving habits, we have wonderful reminders of Padmasambhava in this world:

his holy places to visit, such as in Bhutan (my country of birth) where we have the amazing Paro Taktsang; his mantra and prayers to recite; his statues to look at. And now we have this wonderful book to read and enjoy. Even though the wisdom of the Lotus-Born can't actually be put into words, these letters, words, and stories are the only thing we can relate to at the moment. It is therefore my sincere heartfelt wish that this book will serve as a means of inspiration and mindfulness of this unchanging and sometimes inconvenient truth that Guru Padmasambhava, the Lotus-Born, is embodying in our lives today.

PHONETIC GUIDE

Here is a guide for pronunciation of foreign words in this book. We have tried to be phonetically descriptive for words in Tibetan and Sanskrit while at the same time distinguishing sounds that are pronounced similarly but not exactly the same. In general, vowels are pronounced as in Italian or Spanish. Sanskrit makes a distinction between long and short vowels in the case of *a, i*, and *u*. However, in this text they are not represented differently. Therefore, it is acceptable always to pronounce them as if they were long:

a as in c*a*r.
i as in f*ee*t.
u as in l*oo*t.

The following vowels are always considered long in Sanskrit:

e as in d*ay*
ai as in p*ie*
o as in g*o*
au as in h*ow*

Most consonants are pronounced as in English. The aspirated consonants (*kh, gh, ch, jh, th, dh, ph, bh*) are pronounced as the consonant plus a noticeable aspiration of breath. In particular, note that the consonants *th* and *ph* are not pronounced as in the words *th*ing and *ph*oto, but as in po*th*ole and she*ph*erd. The letter *g* is always pronounced hard as in *g*o, never as in *g*em. The letter *h* is pronounced as a breathing sound at the end of a word.

Bhutan – "boo-tahn"
bodhisattva – "boh-dee-saht-vuh"
Brahmaputra – "brah-mah-poo-truh"
buddha – "boo-duh"
Buddhadharma – "boo-dah-dahr-muh"
dakini – "dah-kee-nee"
Dzongsar Khyentse Rinpoche – "zahng-sahr kyehn-say rihn-poh-shay"
Gautama – "gow-tah-mah"
GURU-PADMA-SIDDHI HUM – "goo-roo pahd-mah sih-dee huhm"
Indrabhuti – "ihn-drah-boo-tee"
Mandarava – "mahn-dah-rah-vuh"
Manjushri – "mahn-joo-shree"
Mutig Tsenpo – "moo-tihg tsehn-poh"
Mutsamey – "moot-sah-may"
naga – "nah-gah"
Namkai Nyingpo – "nahm-kay nyihng-poh"
Nammen Karmo – "nahm-mehn kahr-moh"
Odiyana – "oh-dee-yah-nah"
Padmakara – "pahd-mah-kah-ruh"
Padmasambhava – "pahd-mah-sahm-bah-vuh"

Paro Taktsang – "pah-roh tahk-sahng"
Samye – "sahm-yay"
siddhi – "sih-dee"
Trisong Detsen – "tree-sahng deht-sehn"
Uddiyana – "oo-dee-yah-nuh"
vajra – "vahj-ruh"
Yeshe Tsogyal – "yeh-shay soh-gyehl"
Zahor – "zah-hohr"

PUBLISHER'S NOTE

The life of Padmasambhava is full of magic, otherworldly beings, and spiritual awakening—it is a wild and wonderful ride! The story weaves the tale of the Indian master who established Tantric Buddhism in Tibet, which resulted in a rich and vibrant spiritual tradition that has thrived for over one thousand years.

While many would consider the entire account to be one of folklore, that is not how most Tibetans and Tibetan Buddhists perceive it. The teachings of Tantric Buddhism say that with the mastery of the mind comes the ability to manifest in many ways and that what seems quite impossible to many is actually just a limitation of perception. Also, for the perceiver, the factors of karma, habits, and beliefs shape our "reality" and therefore the idea of different worlds, supernatural beings, and so forth is a reflection of our own state of mind. With this outlook, the marvelous stories of Buddhist masters of the past start to make a lot more sense.

Padmasambhava's life is one of Tibetan Buddhism's most iconic and important stories, so it has long been a dream of mine to help create a book that captures the imagination of future generations, just as the oral, theatrical, and written accounts of it have in the Himalayas for centuries. I approached Sherab Chödzin Kohn to help bring that dream to fruition, and, with a shared sense of inspiration, he poured his heart into this account, finishing his work on it shortly before passing away in early 2020. The stunning art by master Bhutanese painter Thinley Dorji brings the story dazzlingly to life. I couldn't be happier with the result.

While this book was written primarily with children in mind, I find it to be an essential and accessible entry point for people of all ages to connect with the magic and wisdom of this brilliant world.

Ivan Bercholz
Publisher, Bala Kids

Bala Kids
An imprint of Shambhala Publications, Inc.
2129 13th Street
Boulder, Colorado 80302
www.shambhala.com

Text © 2023 by Judith D. Kohn
Illustrations © 2023 by Thinley Dorji

"Seven-Line Supplication to Padmakara" was translated from the Tibetan by the Nālandā Translation Committee under the direction of Vidyadhara the Venerable Chögyam Trungpa Rinpoche. © 1978, 2010 by Diana J. Mukpo and the Nālandā Translation Committee, 1619 Edward Street, Halifax, Nova Scotia B3H 3H9. Used by special permission. All rights reserved.

Cover art: Thinley Dorji
Cover design: Kate Huber-Parker
Interior design: Kate Huber-Parker

All rights reserved. No part of this book may be reproduced in any form or by any means, electronic or mechanical, including photocopying, recording, or by any information storage and retrieval system, without permission in writing from the publisher.

9 8 7 6 5 4 3 2 1

First Edition
Printed in Malaysia

Shambhala Publications makes every effort to print on acid-free, recycled paper.

Bala Kids is distributed worldwide by Penguin Random House, Inc., and its subsidiaries.

Library of Congress Cataloging-in-Publication Data
Names: Chödzin, Sherab, author. | Khyentse, Jamyang, 1961– writer of afterword. | Dorji, Thinley, illustrator.
Title: The magical life of the Lotus-Born / Sherab Chödzin Kohn; afterword by Dzongsar Khyentse; illustrated by Thinley Dorji.
Description: First edition. | Boulder, Colorado: Bala Kids, [2023]
Identifiers: LCCN 2020027658 | ISBN 9781611807851 (hardcover)
Subjects: LCSH: Padma Sambhava, approximately 717–approximately 762—Juvenile literature. | Lamas—Tibet Region—Biography—Juvenile literature.
Classification: LCC BQ7950.P327 C455 2022 | DDC 294.3/923092—dc23
LC record available at https://lccn.loc.gov/2020027658